MARGARET
THE FIRST

ALSO BY DANIELLE DUTTON

Attempts at a Life

SPRAWL

Here Comes Kitty: A Comic Opera (with Richard Kraft)

MARGARET THE FIRST
DANIELLE DUTTON

CATAPULT  NEW YORK

Published by Catapult
Catapult.co

ISBN: 978-1-936787-35-7

Catapult titles are distributed to the trade by
Publishers Group West
Phone: 800-788-3123

Library of Congress Control Number 2015951167

Printed in the United States of America

For Elijah

Art itself is, for the most part, irregular.
—Margaret Cavendish

PROLOGUE

THE WOMAN HAD EIGHT CHILDREN. THE FIRST, CALLED TOM, IN 1603, the final year of Queen Elizabeth's reign. It was five daughters and three sons, and she dressed them richly but simply and cleanly to ward off sharkly habits. Margaret was the youngest. She made the world her book, took a piece of coal and marked a blank white wall. Later, she made sixteen smaller books: untitled, sewn with yarn. Her girlhood heroes were Shakespeare, Ovid, Caesar. She wrote them in beside thinking-rocks and humming-shoes and her favorite sister, Catherine, who starred in all but five. Snow fell fast as she sat by the nursery fire; ink to paper, then she sewed. The last book told a tale of hasty gloom, teeming with many shades of green: emerald, viridian, a mossy black. In it we meet a miniature princess who lives in a seashell castle and sleeps in sheets woven from the eyelids of doves.

For all these fertile inner workings, Margaret was thought plain, couldn't wear yellow, was shy, yes, seemed younger than her years—yet Margaret longed for fame. When grown, she would adorn herself like a peacock. Or so wrote the diarist Samuel Pepys, whose curiosity brought him out one day to stand along a London road and wait for her carriage to pass. It was May Day and the park was like a circus. "The Duchess of Newcastle is all the pageant now discoursed on"—so he'd written in his diary several weeks before. At breakfast tables and dinner parties, over porridge or pike or a gravy made from the brains of a pig, she was all that anyone talked about, as watched for as Queen Catherine herself but a far more thrilling spectacle: those black stars on her cheeks, the scandal at the theater, her hats! One anonymous satirist had dubbed her Welbeck Abbey's illustrious whore. Others called her simply fantastical. An overgrown spoilt girl. Her work: chaos. Her books: sad heaps of rubbish. Voluminous, some called her. Crack-brained. So extremely picturesque. Yet there were others, Pepys knew, who considered her the unequaled daughter of the muses and her latest book a blazing utopia to rival Bacon's own.

He tapped his hat for shade. A crow pecked near his feet. He was about to give it up, and then: "Mad Madge!" someone cried in the street. "Mad Madge!" someone repeated, as her black-and-silver carriage came roaring down the path. But the horses were forced to a stop, for the crowd had grown a mob. "I see her," someone shouted. He saw her then, through the window glass—black stars, white cheeks. That night in his diary he wrote: "The whole story of this lady is a romance, and everything she does."

A TRUE RELATION OF MY
BIRTH AND BREEDING

COLCHESTER TO OXFORD

1623–1644

LEAVING LONDON: THE BUSY ROAD BEFORE US MORPHS TO GORSE
and broom, sheep in grass, cottagers spinning and weaving, till
Colchester looms at last, its Norman castle high above the crumbling Roman wall, and houses scattered down to the River Colne,
the port of the Hythe, the town a full mile from side to side. Colchester—first Camulos, then Camulodunum, some even say it was
Camelot—was famous for its eryngoes: roots of sea holly dug up
like fingers and candied pink or red. Then just outside the walls:
the Lucas estate, St. John's Green. Once the Abbey of St. John the
Baptist, my great-grandfather bought it in 1548 for £132. Dove-
cotes, farmland, a kitchen garden, cows. Over time it was transformed—from monastery to greathouse, from simple green space
to what one visitor would describe as a scene of "rosemary, cut out
with curious order, in satyrs, centaurs, whale and half-men-horses
and a thousand other counterfeited courses." In other words, a

gentleman's estate, the relevant gentleman being Thomas Lucas, my father—so this is where I was born.

With its gable tops and chimneys, gatehouse and stables, queens dined at St. John's Green, where swords and axes shined from walls. Other walls shone with brightly colored silks, windows with damask. Tables were laid with Turkey carpets. And an enormous golden saltcellar stood at the master's right hand— while a master lived, that is. For poor father died unexpectedly one morning as I, his youngest daughter, toddled the garden path. There'd been a party. My second birthday. Orange ribbons twisting down from trees.

AS FOR OUR MOTHER, SHE WAS BEAUTIFUL BEYOND THE RUINS OF time. None of her children would be crooked, of course, nor in any ways deformed. Neither were we dwarfish, or of a giantlike stature, but proportional, with brown hair, sound teeth, sweet breath, and tunable voices—not given to wharling in the throat, I mean, or speaking through the nose, unless we had a cold—yet we were none so prone to beauty as she, and I perhaps least of them all. I had no dimples, my mouth was wide, my hair grew crimped and fierce as wild lettuce from my head.

A SUMMER AFTERNOON, AGE NINE, SITTING FIRST BENEATH FRENCH honeysuckle, then moving nearer the brook to observe butterflies that gather at pale daffodils, a dead sparrow spotted along the way, and a sonnet begun upon the ability of a sparrow to suffer pain, I, Margaret—Queen of the Tree-people—discovered an invisible world. There, on the surface of the water, river-foam bubbles encased a jubilant cosmos. Whole civilizations lasted for only a moment! Yet from the creation of one of these Bubble-worlds to the moment that world popped into oblivion, the Bubble-people within it fell in love, bore children, and died, their bodies decomposing into a fine foamy substance that was then reintegrated into the foamy infrastructure of the world as the Bubble-children grew up and bore children of their own and died and were integrated into the sky and air and water, and even into the furniture, which was itself a fine foamy substance that the Bubble-folk called "coffee." In this world, wild horses ran on open fields and sermonized in church on Sundays, speaking always with great eloquence on vast and noble subjects—such as germination—or giving firsthand descriptions of remote landscapes as seen from the eyes of a running horse: the blur of grasses, wind in the nostrils, how a bee will sometimes bump against your forehead.

Standing at the brook that day, creating and destroying this place via the tip of my new leather boot, I began to contemplate all the creatures I had ever killed—innumerable spiders creeping the nursery floor, beetles and slugs in the kitchen garden, a mouse, once, which startled me as I slept—as well as animals I'd ingested or whose skins I had worn on my hands, head, shoulders, and feet: pigs, cows, rabbits, fox, deer, fish, fowl. Was I, Margaret Lucas, responsible for their deaths if I'd had no hand in the slaughter? By bedtime, I'd decided that I was. And I took care the following Sunday to receive a smaller portion of the roast.

"Picky Peg," my brother teased.

I solemnly chewed my bread.

"Picky Peg," they laughed.

Then I began to weep, openly, into the soup. It wasn't their simple teasing; my mood had been strange all day. For tomorrow I'd be sent to London to visit our sister Mary—my first trip away from home! What if the yellow poppies bloomed? What if our mother died?

That night a storm came tearing through our fields. Perched in the nursery window, I saw the lightning fall in liquid streams. A ghostly army of silhouetted trees fought against the sky! I did not sleep, thinking the weather a terrible portent, and was therefore dressed by dawn—long hair in intricate twists—to breakfast in the dining room attended by my nurse.

The carriage embarked at first light: the sun rose quickly, a teeming of gnats, and all we saw of the previous night's tempest were a few felled trees in the pasture. So, at last, I shut my eyes. I let the carriage lull me. I imagined a floating dinner on a barge upon the Thames . . .

Yet the road to London had been badly pocked by rain. Now one of the horses, a spotted mare, twisted her leg in a rut.

As the driver pulled over to attend the injured animal, I sat and watched the sky—an oceanic mass of gray, with islands of steel blue—thinking, yes, certainly, birds must sleep at times while they fly. How ridiculous it was to think otherwise. Yet my brothers' tutor, a man from Oxford with red eyebrows, had informed me the previous morning that no such thing could occur. Such a thing, he'd opined, would be an affront to God, who had blessed birds with the ability to sleep and the ability to fly, but not the ability to sleep while flying or fly while sleeping. Absurd! Moreover, he went on, were it to be the case, each morning we would find at our feet heaps of dead birds that had smashed into rooftops or trees in the night. Night after night we would be awakened by this ornithological cacophony, this smashing of beaks against masonry, this violence of feathers and bones. It will not do, he said, to too greatly admire the mysteries of nature. But I remembered that sparrow on the riverbank and secretly held that the world was not so easily explained by a tutor's reason. Indeed, it was then that I first formed the opinion—if childishly, idly—that a person should trust to her own good sense and nature's impenetrable wisdom.

What, then, did my own sense tell me when I lowered my eyes to the field and saw a woman, graceless and muddy, emerge from deep within? At first nothing more than a point on the landscape, the stranger walked a line at the carriage until she was stepping through the ragged hedgerow up to the injured horse. Stacks of bracelets on her bare arms clattered. She seemed to have been spun out of gold. At first I was sure it was brave Boadicea, stepping into the roadway as if out of a nursery tale. But the driver urged her off. He called her a Gypsy, a Jew. She paid him no attention, hummed in the horse's ear. And when she approached the carriage, asking for my hand, I, in silent wonder, extended my arm out the door. That lady took it, held it near. "In the not-too-distant future," she finally said, "you will travel by ship to a frozen land. When you return, it will be by night, very late, with sore, tender knees."

ONE MORNING 1 WOKE TO FIND I'D STAINED MY SHEETS AND thought I'd split in two. There followed a quiet clamor: new linens, removal from the nursery, and no one explaining why. Until a maid, in secret, provided useful counsel: Inscribe *veronica* in ink on the ball of your left thumb, to decrease the irksome flow. "Mind you stay out of the kitchen," the maid went on, "as a bleeding girl can turn the sugar black!" Stunned, I fled to my new room, only to find that my mother awaited me inside. "You must wear chicken-skin gloves on your hands each night," my mother began, "for all this wandering picking plums has turned them spotted and brown." I looked down at my hands and saw that change had plainly found me. "When inside the house," my mother went on, "you must not spend all your time writing little books." And she told me, then, the story of Lady Mary Wroth, who'd published a book of fancy two years before my birth and was branded ever after a bearded monster. "Virtue," my mother was saying, "beauty and virtue." Yet out the window, as she spoke, under a net of branches, my youngest brother, Charlie, arrived on the lawn with a hawk. Hood lifted, the hawk flew off. It is nobler to be a boy, I thought—and looked back with nostalgia, as if I just had been.

My new room held two stools, a full bed with bulbous posts, and there was a deep cupboard, newly installed, like a chamber built into the wall. When no one was looking, I sometimes hid inside it. Or else I went in slippers to the gallery, long and narrow and lit by windows with colored heralds that painted the polished wooden floor and paneled walls when the sun shone. Here were cabinets protecting clear Venetian glass, a chiming clock that sang like finches. It was a room of music and gentle motion, where I sat, feet tucked up, in a chair of Spanish leather.

So passed two or three years.

FINALLY SOMETHING HAPPENED, OR ALMOST DID: MARIE DE' MEDICI came to England. Mother to the King of France and Queens of Spain and England, her entourage traveled in style from coast to town, met by crowds in freezing rains, by boys and girls who ran beside the bouncing carriage hoping to spot the famous beauty, by that time splotched and bald.

In Essex she'd be housed at our estate. A tizzy to prepare— our winter trees were leafless. So John, my middle brother, lashed branches from a neighbor's fir onto our barren oaks.

Madame took no notice. Madame was rude. She dribbled diamonds. And she was, I decided, quite impressive.

I curtsied, watched from corners. One lady-in-waiting was especially alluring, wore powder on her hands, rose and sky-blue satin, silver parchment lace like a folded paper fan around her face. There were speeches, drums, a harp and horn. On the final night, they'd dance. I put on a stiff new dress, lace cap, laced boots, my mother's silver openwork brooch—then refused to come out of my room.

When my sisters tried to coax me, I was unable to say why. Bits of lute song rose up through the halls. "Why will you not take more interest in grown-up things?" they asked. It seemed impossible to make myself be any way but wrong. "Baby Peg," my sisters sighed. But I was then sixteen! And when they returned to the party, I escaped to the yard, soothed myself in the branches of an oak tree, dangling over periwinkle, looking out for swifts. *Sixteen*, I reflected, biting into a stolen pie. By this time in her life, my sister Mary had been pregnant. Ovid had dedicated his life to poetry. Queen Elizabeth had seen a suitor beheaded. Romeo and Juliet were dead. Whereas I, Margaret Lucas, was nothing if not in health, no single true adventure to my name.

Of course I did not know then that war was on its way—that Parliament was working to annul the powers of the king, or that the king would raise his royal battle standard in return. I did not know that by that summer my brother John would have a stockpile of weapons stashed inside our house.

One morning that June, I took only a conserve of marigolds for breakfast, trying to loosen a cough, and, after wandering the halls, went to the garden with two hard plums in my pocket. I ate; the church bell tolled. Eventually, in petal-flecked shoes, I found my way to the sitting room, where my mother dozed and John's pregnant wife stood absently by the settle. The room was remarkably hot, for Mother believed in keeping windows shut, and a fat summer fly bumped against the glass. I stood at a table fiddling with a vase. I counted thirty-seven stems and dreamt up a ruby coat for a Chinese empress, a watery dress for Ophelia, a series of towering crystalline hats that rattled, sparkled, and shook—until from the hall came a series of noises. A shout, a bump, boots on stone. The door was flung open, and all at once, twenty men were standing on the carpet.

They smelled of sweat and hay, their faces half-covered or angry and red. The scene seemed frozen, like a painting on the wall, as from the darkened hallway came a pillow of cool air. Then one man put his sword to my sister-in-law's neck and demanded she give up her husband, the guns. My sister-in-law fainted. My mother awoke. They stood us on the lawn.

They were Parliamentarians, of course, though I did not understand. And they apprehended my brother, too, or else he gave himself up.

We were all four marched to the Colchester jail, John's wife weak and breathless, as hundreds of angry citizens shouted at us from the fields.

This was on a Monday. On Friday they let us go.

We reached the house early, to doors hanging open, mud and leaves on the floor. The mob had slaughtered the deer in Lucas Park, stripped and beaten our parson, driven off our cows. Money and jewels were gone, furniture stolen, our garden walls pulled down. Each night for nights I could not sleep, convinced they would return. Our neighbors, our tenants: I feared they'd drink our blood. For that mob had even broken into the family vaults and—with pistols, swords, and halberds—defiled the coffins and the corpses of our dead.

WAS IT FROM SHOCK, THEN, OR FEAR, OR A NAÏVE SENSE OF CIVIC duty that I asked to join the queen's court at Oxford? Certainly, the stories were remarkable. One: that French-born Queen Henrietta Maria (Marie de' Medici's daughter) had scandalized the English by acting in her own court masques—now a princess, now an Amazon, now a water nymph, and so on. Two: that the glamorous young queen, fond of masquerades even offstage, had roamed along the Thames and through riverside meadows, disguised, in order to look upon the haymakers, and even take up a pitchfork and make hay. Three: that the queen, calling herself She-Majesty Generalissima, led an army from Bridlington to Oxford, straddling her horse like Alexander and eating with the men in the field.

Or had I simply spotted my way out?

Upon hearing the queen had fewer ladies in Oxford than she'd been used to in London, hands at my sides, before a painting of a dog, I requested of my mother that I be allowed to go. "I have," I said, "a great desire to do so." My sisters were against it. I'd embarrass myself, the family. Mary insisted it would be kinder to me *not* to let me go.

"Surely you see," wrote Anne from London, "dear Margaret is eccentric—more apt to read than dance. Why does she never smile? And why does her hat seem never to match her gown?"

"Consider," whispered John's wife, "she's been so infrequently from home."

"I'd not be surprised," Catherine wrote, "if she still hunts satyrs and fairies at every summer moon."

But this war had come like a whirlwind. Our mother was afraid. I'd be safer at Oxford, she decided, than alone in the country at home, thus she rang for me one morning and consented to my plan.

KISSES ON THE LAWN AT ST. JOHN'S GREEN. A PERFECT SUMMER gloom of vegetal bravado: peonies, bugloss, native beetles singing. The horses stamped a path through the starry dark. Alone in the carriage, flying through England, I imagined myself a beauty in satin; I imagined a crown of diamonds on my head; I imagined I'd soon be married to a celebrated general, but that days after the wedding my husband would fall in battle, so that I, in a silver coat to my waist, with a broad sword in my hand, would have no choice but to rally his troops and lead them onto the field; I imagined a royal reception, the road strewn with petals, bells.

But the coach stopped the following night in an obscure and narrow lane. The horses slobbered, a squat door opened, and I was sped inside, a strange man gripping my elbow. It was a baker's home, a safe house. I did not sleep, kept my wits. Amid the city's tolling bells, the smell of yeast and mold, I crept to the window and saw a stack of soldiers' bodies.

Morning brought another man, rain, a series of crowded hallways, then around a corner and I stood before the queen—the queen!—stunning and Catholic and dressed in red and ermine. Dozens of silent courtiers stood pressed against the walls. But it was as if I'd watched it all unfold within a book, as if I turned the pages from safe inside my room: the dead soldiers, the baker's house, the courtiers, the queen. Until someone whispered, "How simple she looks," and all at once I awoke.

I found myself in an unknown universe, whirling far into space: African servants, dogs in hats, platonic ideals, sparkling conversation, and ivy-coated quadrangles with womanizing captains, dueling earls, actors. I met Father Cyprien de Gamache, her majesty's wily confessor; William, a poet, who claimed to be Shakespeare's son; and a giggling dwarf called Jeffry, who'd been presented to the queen in a pie. I met the ladies-in-waiting, too, who hardly looked my way, busy as they were, bickering over who went where and when, who wore what and when, who fetched what and why, who said what and to whom, and what gave *her* the right to say *that*. Nor was Oxford itself at all what I'd expected: dead horses clogged the waterways, corpses from both sides were flung on Jews' Mount. Grain was stored in Law & Logic, boots cobbled in the School of Astronomy & Music. At the center of it all, the queen, newly pregnant, rarely left her makeshift palace, and I, as one of her ladies-in-waiting, waited each day by her side. With downcast eyes, I minded her fan. I minded her red fox train.

Worst of all: I was permanently underdressed, in my older sisters' outmoded hand-me-downs and caps. So I designed in my mind a sugar-spun golden gown to walk the path to church in, trailing crimson flowers and greenish beetle wings. Then someone cupped my breasts—two-handed!—as I passed like a ghost down the hall. I never spoke, but immediately sent word to my mother, begging to be allowed back home. "It is a mistake," I wrote, "and not where I belong." Mother as promptly refused. Bad as I thought I had it, life outside was swiftly unraveling for those still loyal to the king. "Be tranquil," her note advised, "this war will soon be over."

But the following spring it was not.

IN HIDING AT A ROYALIST ESTATE IN EXETER—THE SEA, THE AIR, THE double white violet, the wallflower, stock-gilliflower, cowslip, flower-de-lices, cherry trees in pink—the queen gave birth to a princess, soft and yellow, streaked with blood, the labor causing hysterical blindness and a lingering pain in Her Majesty's chest.

THE CHANNEL TO PARIS

1644–1645

TO BEGIN CAME AN ATTACK BY PARLIAMENTARIAN SHIPS—THE *VICE Admiral*, *Warwick*, and *Paramour*—just off the coast of Devon. Cannons fantastically loud! Then French ships sailed out to meet us and the Parliamentarians quickly fled, so we unfurled the purple banners—*Long live the King*—but rough winds blew us westward into storms.

The ship pitched, banging doors. England disappeared.

In one small cabin six beds hung like cradles from a beam, and beneath my own a barrel of beans was home to a mischief of rats. My cabinmates were sick, vomiting into chamber pots they took on deck to dump. I sat and watched the sea exhaust itself out a circular glass, swells as high as any hill in Essex. If light allowed, I read. *Twelfth Night* in a gale. Would Viola's fate be mine, washed ashore in a strange new world and dressed up like a man? I tucked up my feet and waited, swinging in the bed.

But no wreck came. Nor were we mistaken for pirates by fishermen out at dawn. We rowed ashore, at last, on the rocky coast of Brittany, struggled up a cliff. Next, by land, passing monks and bullocks and avenues of walnuts. We stopped in Bourbon to catch our breath, walk our spaniels. An ancient château sat over a monastery and a warm medicinal spring, where the queen soaked, finches whistling, as French physicians pierced her abscessed breast. Finally, in November, queen and court reached Paris, where the Regent of France, on behalf of the six-year-old king, had granted us use of the Louvre. I read, sticking to Spenser and Donne. "She is unsociable," the others said, "and cannot grasp French." I paced the cloister, the bells of Notre Dame clanging in the distance. I read. I wrote letters to my mother and sisters. And idly one afternoon, I wrote something else:

"I had rather be a meteor, singly, alone."

Plus Paris itself was noisome. Even with its glittering bridges and orangeries, even if the birthplace of ballet.

"I had rather been a meteor, than a star in a crowd."

There was the humidity, the innumerable crashing coaches, and French aristocrats and servants relieving themselves in the halls. All summer, heaps of shit steamed on the palace steps. I swear I nearly died of the purging flux that August, saved by a powder of opium, pearls, and gold taken in a bread-pill each night before I slept.

O the fever. The dreams!

Yet most of all, I was bored—*so* bored. Having arrived at the height of history, the very middle of the world, I was shocked to find myself with less to do than when alone in the country back home. Though marbled and with warbling fountains, the Louvre was vast and always cold. As ladies-in-waiting schemed down endless mirrored corridors, the once-luminous queen retreated, weeping, desperate for the baby she'd been forced to leave in England—safe from the perils of our escape. Some days it seemed as if my fever had never broken: the incessant pointless duels, those ghostly caryatids, a monkey in a doublet roaming halls. Too, I'd grown aware of some new flimsiness in my body—stretching out my long thin arms, the skin as light as muslin, as likely to rip or tear. Even weeks after my illness, my face was white as clay. I refused to run, refused to break a sweat. While ladies-in-waiting pranced and spun, gave chase to honking swans, I only sat and watched them from the knotted flower beds, ignored the book in my lap, and recalled the grounds at St. John's Green: the fields of purpling wild lettuce, the spidery fern-ringed pond.

Then one downcast afternoon, as I approached my shaded bench, I saw a woman, tall even seated, broad-shouldered and tanned, yet elegantly gowned in gray and pearl ropes. It was a peculiarly informal meeting: I simply sat. My stiff skirts brushed that lady's, and I opened my book in silence. Yet despite this odd behavior, she took pity on a hushed and sighing girl. "My Mary," she said, pointing to a child amid the topiary shapes, "who was ten this past July."

Thus, in a tonsured garden, near a wall of autumn roses, it happened that I made a friend—my first. Lady Browne was newly arrived from London, wife of Sir Richard, French ambassador for our king. Soon I was a regular at their home.

AT THE EMBASSY FOR SUPPER—QUAIL IN BROTH AND OYSTERS—LADY Browne remembered my father, whom she'd met at Queen Elizabeth's court. Yet one name only was on the tongue of Sir Richard: William Cavendish, newly made marquess. This gentleman, he reported between oysters, had recently fled to Hamburg after losing badly with a regiment raised near York. A master horseman and fencer, and one of the richest men in England, he wrote plays—oyster—collected viols—oyster—"his particular love in music"—and was by all accounts—oyster—affable and quick. As for official news, the post arrived on Tuesdays. I was sometimes sent to retrieve it from a sympathetic banker in the Rue de Quiquempoit. The queen employed secret couriers for her letters to the king, transported to Oxford in wigs or hollow canes. If apprehended, well, the agents risked death. By now it was clear: the Royalists were losing.

AND THOUGH AWKWARD STILL IN THE PRESENCE OF ANY MAN WHO wasn't a brother, yet I appear in a painting from around this time— of the queen and her exiled ladies—with my neckline plunging deep, as was the mode: I wear a cherry cap, have good plump breasts, fair skin, precise little curls.

IN 1645 WILLIAM CAVENDISH ARRIVED IN PARIS IN A COACH PULLED BY nine Holsteiner horses. In truth, the marquess had run out of funds but rightly assumed he'd get better credit if he seemed a less risky investment, so presented himself to the queen and gave her a gift of six of his steeds. Henrietta Maria accepted on the panoramic steps of the Louvre. Ladies-in-waiting in springtime flounces flanked her. William's seasoned eye lighted on one whose own, this once, looked back. What was that shy girl thinking? That standing in velvet on freshly raked gravel was a version of Shakespeare or Caesar? Here indeed was manly fame and fortune: a playwright and poet, a horseman and soldier, a handsome widower and infamous flirt. But would he ask to meet her, the girl with the quiet stare, sister of one of his captured commanders? There were many unmarried ladies at court: some of them rich, quite a few pretty, each hoping to make a good match. William Cavendish had his pick. He picked me, to wide surprise.

Firstly, he existed in a social sphere far above my own. And I, who rarely spoke, almost never spoke to men. But at thirty years my senior, William knew—unlike noisy young courtiers—how to seduce a strange bright virgin. He watched me in my silence. My reserve? He thought it charming. His attentions made me blush. I could feel his stare as I snuck off with *Cymbeline* to a corner. "You enjoy reading?" he asked. We walked the courtyard under jealous eyes. He spoke of things that mattered—my brother, books, my home—and had a way of standing, feet spread, so that his brown eyes met my green ones at one level. Then, and wisely, he began to frequent the embassy, where we often met on Sundays, he kneeling beside me, watching my lips move as I prayed. I was to him a new-come bud, so slender and pale. I smelled of roses, or so he said. I turned pink and asked about my brother.

But just as I began to soften, Henrietta Maria up and quit Paris, taking herself and her court to St. Germain-en-Laye. Her summer château boasted grand suites with painted windows and formal gardens descending to the Seine, with canals and cascading fountains and a cove of faux-grottoes home to clacking metal birds, a bejeweled caterpillar, a golden duck that shook its head and quacked. We smuggled letters. Like clockwork, William composed one poem every other day. I was a "spotless virgin, full of love and truth." My breasts so plump and young. "If living cannot meet," wrote he,

> *then let us try*
> *If after death we can; oh let us die!*

And I: "I look apon this world as on a deths head for mortifi-cashun, for I see all things subject to allteration and change, and our hopes as if they had takin opium."

And he:

> *Sweetest of nature, virtue, you are it;*
> *Serenest judgement, fancy for a wit;*
> *So confidently modest, so discreet,*
> *As lust turns into love, love homage at your feet.*

Summer scorched. Fires burned in surrounding fields posting towers of smoke between the château and Paris. But poetry toils, even in such heat. By the end of the summer, William and I were secretly engaged. Unaccustomed, I troubled. William, brave in secrecy, pressed me against a wall, hands working to get under all those skirts. I hurried down the corridor, locked myself in my room. Alone on the bed, I wished my mother borne across the sea, in through the open painted window, standing on the cold stone floor in France, as if by magic. As others lunched in a tent on the grass, I wrote another note, begging he be patient: "If you shod repent sir how unfortunat a woman I shod be; pray consider I have enemyes."

It was true! A swelling noise arose at court, the ladies in a rage. Some said coy Miss Lucas had played the marquess like a song. Others whispered loudly about his numerous past lovers and a rumored decline in stamina. His closest friends opposed the match. I had no dower, the war having taken my family's wealth. I was of gentle but unremarkable birth. I was odd, that much was obvious, even to idle courtiers. They made no attempt to hide what they said, and soon a different rumor reached me: that the marquess courted another. Naturally, I panicked. I even began to admire Paris because William was in it: "Shurly, my lord," I wrote in haste, "I shall be content to be any thing you would have me to be, so I am yours; I rejoyce at nothing mor than your leters."

I needn't have despaired.

One day by the river's edge he stuck his tongue in my mouth. Unsure, I tugged it with my lips and nearly choked him. An afternoon while others played *boules* on the grass, he took me for a ride and pinched my nipples. Then it happened: someone leaked our secret to the queen. Her own maid-in-waiting? A *nobody* in her house? Henrietta Maria swore she'd faint. She called for a glass of wine, declared the chapel hot. And I, immediately struck by another summer fever, kept to my chamber the remainder of the season.

WHEN PRINCESS MARIE OF MANTUA MARRIED THE ANCIENT KING OF Poland (incontinent and crippled by gout), all Paris lined the streets to watch: mounted soldiers in Turkish jackets, their horses' skin dyed red; footguards in yellow regalia; Polish *seigneurs* in a wealth of jewels, despite a lack of taste. Madame de Motteville reported that the foreigners slept in animal skins and wore no underclothes, but *how she knew* was what got everybody talking.

Amid this din, Margaret Lucas became Margaret Cavendish in the ambassador's private Parisian chapel. It was autumn. I wore gray. My hair in waves around my face and braided up at back. No other Lucas could be present, but Lady Browne fondly shed a sister's worth of tears, and her daughter Mary carried a myrtle bouquet. Then out to the waiting carriage—horses stamping slick with rain—where William swiftly handed me up and sat down beside me, his wife.

So began our journey, our life. But what does one say? What do? William sat in silence. I watched him warily from the edges of my sight. Had I erred? My thoughts slid over the morning as the embassy raced from view: my arrival, the vows, the giving of rings, the proclamation, the blessings. But no, I'd hardly said three words. And with another glance—his salt-and-pepper beard, his broad-brimmed hat—I clicked through stories I'd read or heard, of husbands, cruel and cold, who changed after the wooing. One who was handsome but mean. One who never listened. One who threatened to boil his lady's pug in a pot. Then William turned to face me. He took my hands from my lap. "My circumstances in exile," he began, "my situation, you see, is not what it is back home." And my fingers relaxed in his. I was far more worried about causing offense than being offended myself.

In England, as I surely knew—"Damned awkward to speak of money, and yet"—in England he could boast two noble estates. There was Welbeck Abbey in Nottinghamshire—with its avenue of fir trees and swans upon the lake—where he was Marquess of Newcastle and I now Marchioness. And not a day's ride to the west sat the ancient castle of Bolsover, on a gentle slope, turreted and thick with scented vines. "Once," he said, "I spent £20,000 entertaining the king for a week. What quantities of wine we drank and game we shot!" But now, well. In France, you see. "In short," William said, "I'm poor." *Poorish*.

Too, in certain circles, in certain courtly circles, among certain younger courtiers, "I'm thought of these days as a bit of an also-ran, a nit." The troops he'd commanded so thoroughly routed at Marston Moor, where my brother had been captured. "Damn Scots!" William spat, and I diverted my gaze to low-hanging wooden signboards swinging over shops. It had not been any error of his. Details would emerge. History would know his worth. "To come to the matter," he said, "our situation *will* improve." There was no point at all on which I should trouble myself. Only steel my ears against gossip. This war would soon be over.

Then a bang of thunder upset the horses and the carriage began to tip—around a corner with two wheels on the ground, water creeping in through seams—a dive! a plunge! a sag! a wreck!—but all was right in seconds, all four wheels on the ground. A current of wet Parisians passed outside the glass. "For now," he said, replacing his fallen hat, "we will live in the rented wing of a house, yet a graceful château and just beyond the city gate."

As if on cue, that gate appeared, damp and gray as all Paris, my dress. A regiment of birds strutted blackly at its base. Rain, rain, as far as the eye could see. A drop fell into my lap.

It was: the gate, those crows, some soggy lindens, a fountain, and I was home.

NEXT, A WHIRLWIND OF DETAIL: SERVANTS IN A LINE, EACH WITH A name and position to remember. I curtsied one by one, and William had to wait. Now came faces of his family and friends, to whom I gave shy greeting. He led me by the hand. I saw high-backed chairs with lion's-paw feet, exposed beams in the hall, then lifted my skirts and mounted the staircase to a long and narrow corridor, where he kissed me with my back against a door. Satisfied, he turned, the tip of his sheathed sword sliding down the wall, off to join the others in a toast.

The room was smaller than the one I'd been used to at the Louvre, yet all my own, and neat and clean, with bright white walls and two tall windows that watched a narrow street. Should I sit? Take off my cap? *Margaret Cavendish*, I thought, *will now take off her cap*.

Then, like a ghost, a little maid appeared. A little maid in bright white muslin who didn't say a word, only stripped away the bridal gown and washed my new-wife's skin—with rough French hands, French soap—and touched my breasts and thighs with tuberose perfume.

Dripping cold and naked, I thought: *William, Willy, Wally, Bill.*

It was the century of magnificent beds. Beds like ships from China, or beaded purses, in black and white, or pearled. Beds that disappeared behind a cloud of scented silk. Now an elaborately embroidered brocade curtain exposed my arm, an elbow. I heard their toasts from down below, voices muffled through wood and plaster, just as the world had sounded from my nursery as a girl. I could picture William exactly as I'd first seen him: standing in velvet on freshly raked gravel. It had been only that spring! Then an afternoon, not three months after, when the riverbank was muddy and he'd held me very close. He'd wanted to speak of nothing but me. "A strange enchantment," I told him. "As if I live in the world but also somehow out." For he should know I'd always been this way. "But you're not yet twenty," he'd said with a smile. "But I'm nearly twenty-two."

The maid was gone. An Epithalamium played. William opened the door.

His skin was papery. Pleasant, I thought, but papery, loose.

That evening I wrote my mother that he gave me combs and bracelets; William wrote a poem:

> *To say we're like one snake, not us disgraces,*
> *That winds, delights itself, with self-embraces,*
> *Lapping, involving, in a thousand rings.*

Naturally the talk at dinner was pebbled with first-night jokes. And though seasoned by my time at court, I felt my cheeks go red. I didn't speak, just sipped and chewed: roasted carp, claret, a shoulder of mutton with thyme, and a fine sugar cake with sprigs of candied rosemary like diamonds. William saw nothing amiss in the banter; his wife was young and very lately a virgin, and his house a household of men.

There was his brother, Sir Charles, with a twisted spine and auburn mustache, considered in certain circles a great philosopher; William's grown sons from his first marriage, Henry and Charles (called Charlie like my brother); William's steward; William's secretary; William's gentleman of the horse; William's "man"; William's ushers, who walked bareheaded before him when he went out. There were female servants, too, and the usual rumors. Over them all, I, Lady Cavendish, now presided. To varying degrees, each ignored me.

PARIS TO ANTWERP

1646–1649

WHEN LONDON INTELLECTUAL JOHN EVELYN MARRIED LADY
Browne's now-twelve-year-old Mary, William and I were among
the selected guests. My husband, ever lyrical when it came to virgins, wrote a poem for Evelyn comparing his wife to a horse.

Autumn again, and we attended the opera: Rossi's *Orfeo* at the
Palais Royale.

At court: there was a masque that Christmas.

On the Pont Neuf: barges on the Seine (do fishes in the river
miss the salt of the sea?).

Before a painting: the *femme forte*, a woman dressed in armor.

In spring, at the ballet: a spectacle of satin.

At the Tuileries: caged tigers lit by torches.

And being fitted: many yards of colored ribbon.

At home: our house was a salon, William a world-class host.
He was witty, laughed easily, set everyone at ease. He was, too, I
quickly learned, a rather famous patron—of Dryden, Gassendi,

Jonson, and more. I greeted with practiced curtsies, grasped a Chinese fan. Here came William Davenant, poet laureate, who'd lost his nose to syphilis and wore a black cloth in its place. Handsome Lord Widdrington, Bishop John Bramhall, Edmund Waller with his fishy eye, Sir Kenelm Digby, and merry Thomas Hobbes. As for the French: René Descartes, Roberval, and the father of acoustics, Marin Mersenne, who stared openly at my breasts.

Of what did they speak as they stood or sat near the fire?

In the beginning they came to eat; William was generous, even when insolvent, and many of the exiles had fled with nothing but their shirts. On the buffet sat wine, cheeses hard and soft, bread, poached apples, berries or asparagus, fish with horseradish, sliced salted ham.

A man from Japan folded paper into frogs.

An Austrian played *rondeaux* upon the harpsichord.

One evening someone asked what modern scheme would replace the collapsed Aristotelian system, the Middle Ages with their air, wind, earth, and fire, their Ptolemaic structure of the heavens. Soon, beside empty glasses and snuffboxes, strange homemade instruments materialized on our tables: telescopes, compasses, captoptics, more. They spoke of new philosophies, in English or French, of bustling worlds in microscopes, the human body and mind, atomic operations and mechanical arrangement. It was all perfectly new to my thinking. I'd never seen a barometer, or cupped a lens in my palm. I sat in the corner, pretending to read or sew.

One especially spirited night, William himself proposed that each star we see is a sun, with planets above and below. "It stands to reason," he explained, "that the universe is filled with planets we cannot perceive, due to the strength of their suns. Invisible, you see, yet teeming with life." "Yes, if—" someone started; "No, but—"

another broke in. Lively debate ensued, and a newcomer, seeing me listen, asked me for my thoughts. I demurred, claiming my sex as reason. A second man then sportingly suggested they debate the nature of woman. "You will find, sir," I abruptly spoke, "women as difficult to be known and understood as the universe." The room fell silent. I was surprised as any man. Madame de La Fayette called the following week.

Indeed I was, for the very first time, totally *à la mode*. Talk of the place and role of women had been circulating through fashionable salons in each district of the city. Sex a physical distinction, not a quality of mind? A writer, they insisted, must be totally unique. What shape are the atoms at the bottom of the sea? The language of the universe is music. No, math! Hobbes insisted he'd been first to attain a theory of light. Descartes rejected any bodily perception. Someone claimed the right kind of ship might as easily sail *up* as east. You cannot move from "I am thinking" to "I am thought." Passions flared. William stood in the middle, attempting to keep peace. I listened from my chair or upstairs in my room. As quickly as I'd entered their conversation, I slipped out of it again. My mind, I often felt, was like a little cave of mud. I never spoke to Master Hobbes, said nothing to Descartes. In fact—William couldn't fail to notice—his wife spoke less and less.

In March, in London, my niece died from consumption. In April, my sister Mary. In Ireland that summer my brother Tom was crushed by his horse. The following autumn, our mother was taken.

Alone in my room in Paris, I felt oblivion creep near.

I wrote: "Mother liv'd to see the ruin of her Childrin in which was her ruin and then died."

I wrote: "I did a silent mourning Beautie spy."

TWO YEARS OF MARRIAGE PASSED AND STILL I WAS NOT PREGNANT. Remedies were prescribed, everything from more rest to the excrement of a virile ram rubbed across my belly. The king's own doctor, Sir Theodore Mayerne, wrote to William from London: Was the marquess aware that a woman could not conceive without an excited swelling, a heat? Of what frequency and duration was my ardor? A French doctor insisted that William need only lift my spirits, for a woman cannot get pregnant if she is always sad. I had taken to regular vomits, refused to come out of mourning, refused the doctor's tinctures, which gave me terrible gas. Yes, I was often quiet, as the doctor had observed. But my husband chose not to worry. That summer I turned twenty-four.

Then William's son Henry died. Or, he nearly died. He lay near death in England. Letters rushed to Paris, each contradicting the others. His doctors flushed him with gold and mercury. They dusted powdered frog on his meat at every meal. Still, he worsened.

William troubled in the garden. He troubled atop his horse.

And though Henry was only a second son, I was under an ever-increasing pressure to produce. Each night we tried again. Each morning I asked for the carriage and made the daily tour: down the expansive Cour de la Reine, seeing all of fashionable Paris without, myself, being seen.

Bien sûr, they knew I was in there. I was Margaret Cavendish, marchioness, hiding in her carriage.

Yet as Paris whispered of my failure, my husband, over fifty, was buying tonic on the sly: one for *elevating*, made of the backbones of vipers, to be taken half-a-dram each day dissolved in broth. That same French doctor urged mutton dressed with new-laid eggs and a little nutmeg or amber. He advised my husband to anoint his big toes in Spanish oil each night.

On top of all this, our money was gone. Parisian creditors were anxious and would not provide: no meat, no wine, no wax. I was tormented by worries William would be thrown in debtor's jail. Fortunately, the queen, conscious of an obligation, finally repaid a sizable loan that William had made her in Yorkshire. He promptly bought two Barbary horses, one telescope from Torricelli, and four from Divini's shop. "More important than baguette," he said, "is to maintain the *appearance* of means." In the mornings I stood in a nearby grove, thinking of my dead mother, transfixed by the peeling bark. Each night we tried again. Each day I called for the carriage. The crowds. The doctor came. Then a letter arrived from London with news that Henry had recovered, was up out of his bed. Still, I felt more suited to sitting on graves than dancing at Christmas balls. Invitations came, but I turned them down. At New Year's William's telescopes reached us in boxes packed with straw. There was even one for me, in fine marbled paper, a gift. "My Lady's Multiplying Glass," he said, and taught me how to hold it up a breath away from my eye.

Thus as a family—frustrated, gassy, impotent, poor—we wondered together at the turning of the stars.

PALE YELLOW SPIDERS SPECKED OUR TINY PARISIAN GARDEN—*LIKE Cassiopeia on a leaf,* I thought, *and there is the Harp, the Crab*—when one mild afternoon the ambassador came to call. The Scots, he explained, had raised a regiment for the king. Now Prince Charles was off to Rotterdam, to better prepare to return, and the queen wanted William to follow, to help keep her boy secure.

Packing, packing, servants, horses.

I swear, I nearly floated out of town.

Four long years, now free. Free of Paris's piss-stink alleys and constant doctor visits, its mindless idle gossip and endless gray construction. True, it wasn't a return to the grassy fields of home, yet travel through the Low Countries afforded golden views: huge sky meeting flattest land, windmills in sunbeams, cows! Each time we approached a town I'd marvel again at the streets—so wide and clean—and masts of boats peeking above a rainbow of Dutch houses.

As our carriages trundled north, and barking dogs and children ran into the lane to watch, I tried to imagine what life would be now: Rotterdam on the Rotte, a port. Beyond that: an empty room. I pulled my cloak around myself. The houses were lit like lanterns. The farmers heading in. I felt a hopeful kind of sadness, driving down that road. I prayed the war would end—in a day, a month, a week—so that we could live at Welbeck Abbey, where I knew he longed to be. I could be a proper wife. Have my sisters to visit. The children in their beds, I thought. Peacocks on the lawn.

But by the time we reached Rotterdam, Prince Charles had disappeared. With money from his brother-in-law he'd put together a fleet. Sail north! Save the king! There was trouble, though: his ship was late, and troops in Scotland refused to march south without him; the battle at Preston easily went to Cromwell.

Yet another battle, in Colchester, my home, was not so simply won. The city was surrounded, the struggle protracted, until one night with roaring drums Parliamentarian forces broke through a Royalist blockade. Fighting ensued at St. John's Green. The house was destroyed, flattened. Our family vaults were again invaded, but this time it was my sister's and mother's coffins the mob defiled. Rings from their fingers stolen, their arms flung into gardens, their legs splashed into the pond. One Royalist report swore Parliamentarian soldiers rode off with the dead ladies' hair in their hats. Still, the siege lasted another two months. My youngest brother, Charlie, commanded the Royalist forces. The townspeople ate cats and horses. A beggar woman tried to flee and was stabbed at the gates. No one could come out as long as the traitors were in. At last, the Royalists surrendered. Rank-and-file were drawn and quartered. The officers placed themselves at Parliament's mercy. Charlie was shot in the head.

When word reached Rotterdam, I collapsed on the floor. Since leaving England, I'd lost two brothers, one sister, a niece, and a much-loved mother. My childhood home, the place I'd been happiest—for I was happy then, wandering pastures, picking plums, writing my childish poems, I was happy, I was sure—was gone, my mother's body strewn across its park. The Lucas clan, once so close-knit, was now completely unraveled, and I had come to believe myself incapable of procreation, of mending those gaping holes with tiny people of my producing. In bed at night I cried out that I was drowning. In that city of water and dams I dreamt of shipwreck every night.

"A damp sponge," I mumbled.

"All rubble," I said. "All rubble."

A doctor came and bled me till I calmed.

HE'D BEEN THERE BEFORE—TO VISIT THE RYKERS, HARPSICHORD makers, renowned for the lifelike insects painted on their soundboards—and liked what he had seen: large houses, country estates, superior art collections. Provincial, yes, but affordable, quiet, *and she needs to be somewhere quiet*, so leaving his wife in the housekeeper's care, William rode south to Antwerp—fast through browns, through greens, the horizon and the distant city fading into white. All this he later described: how at sundown he stabled his horse, and that night at the inn, over drumsticks with sage, heard the widow of Peter Paul Rubens was looking to let the late painter's house.

IN BLACK BENEATH THE POTTED LIME TREES, AN ARBOR HEAVY WITH roses, I listened as the cathedral with its lacy spire chimed at every hour, south to the reedy countryside, north to the sea, over monasteries with stained glass, over Antwerp's clean broad streets and the leading publishing house in Europe—printing in Syriac, Hebrew, even musical notes—over lindens and canals and savage-looking orchids. It could have easily fit inside one wing of William's estate at Welbeck, yet all who saw the Rubens House agreed it was a gem: vaulted windows, colorful frescoes, rooms half-paneled and hung with Flemish leather. He gave me a tortoiseshell cabinet bound with gold, an ebony comb for my hair. He stood in the riotous Renaissance courtyard waving his hat and smiling. I waved back from two floors up, my chamber domed in blue, windows to a columned pavilion, tulips and low hedges.

Eventually, I took to the carriage and established a daily tour: past the East India Company, the Palace of Oosterhuis, boats upon the Scheldt. With fewer people to look at than in Paris, also fewer by whom to be seen, I took pleasure in the rows of tiny shops, the salty air. Here were ladies wearing feathered hats, children eating fried potato in the street. I stopped to watch an Italian troupe perform in the market square. I'd never seen a woman play a man before. How beautiful that lady-husband in her vest and red silk tights, how graceful when she swung her sword and plunged.

Yet some nights I woke with William beside me and thought for a moment he was my dead brother Tom. "Is this me?" I whispered. How did I come to be here? I remembered the tiny shops, the children in the street. All this, I thought in darkness, is temporary. The sun. The salty air. Everything will stop, for me, except myself. I, Margaret, singular, alone. And on he slept.

THE KING OF ENGLAND WAS CONVICTED OF TREASON. THEN THE King of England was dead. It was Tuesday. It was 1649. Parliament hacked off Charles I's head outside the Banqueting House at Whitehall. The mob, previously sick for it, drew quiet after the blow. The people were burdened with heavy taxes. May Day had been replaced by zealous sermons. Was the Civil War now over? Stunned, no one was sure.

DAYS LATER THE DEAD KING'S SON—NOW CHARLES II—WAS
crowned King of England at The Hague. William stood by him
for the oath, then limped south to Antwerp, which I described in
a letter to my sister as "the most pleasantest and quietest place to
retyre himself and ruin'd fortunes inn."

ANTWERP

1649-1651

AFTER WINTER CAME SPRING, AFTER SPRING THE HEAT OF SUMMER. William was officially banished, his estates officially seized, and I, officially, was not pregnant. This time they tried, for him, crystals taken from wood ash and dissolved in wine each morning; for me, a tincture of herbs put into my womb at night with a long syringe. I submitted silently, William out in the hall. Come autumn I was to be injected in my rectum with a decoction of flowers one morning, followed by a day-long purge, using rhubarb and pepper, then a day of bleeding, then two days where I took nothing but a julep of ivory, hartshorn, and apple, followed by another purge— and on the seventh day I rested. After this came a week of the steel medicine (steel shavings steeped in wine with fern roots, nephritic wood, apples, and more ivory), described by a maid as "a drench that would poison a horse." Then summer again: all fizzy spa water and aniseed candies, and motion and rest, in pre- scribed degrees, and partridge for dinner, or mutton—but never lettuce!—and once a week a bath perfumed with mallows before I slept. If I developed hemorrhoids, I should place leeches on them or be bled from the thigh. And above all else, the doctor said, I must try to be cheerful. No one conceives when sad, he reminded. But I wasn't sad, exactly, not sad only; I was busy.

Sick of filling days with treatments and reproaches, William and I were finding a way that suited us. Rather than apply leeches to my hemorrhoids, in the afternoons I sat under the roses, listening as if I had no other thoughts as he talked or joked or lectured on generals or laws or war, spoke of anatomy, trade, architecture, and colonization, famous statesmen, the rise of nations, the tyranny of kings, the righteousness of kings, the pastimes of kings, of religion, famous poets and their merits, the shapes of atoms, the diets of peoples around the world. We spoke of music. He took me to hear a master violist. It seemed I could remember every word he spoke. "It is," I said, "as if a misty stupor lifts."

Meanwhile, though pleased by my progress, William grew restless for himself. He wrote two plays in quick succession, then decided to transform the late painter's studio into a riding school. Indeed, he was a clever horseman. Ben Jonson, seeing him at manège, once said: "I begin to wish myself a horse!" Naturally the school was a sensation, William in high demand. More and more, therefore, I found myself alone. Yet before I could begin to drift into the reeds, William's brother, Sir Charles, returned from southern travels, and I found I had two dazzling masters instead of one.

Charles was trying to square the circle. He was constructing an equation to determine the outcome of desire plus fear, the evolution from emotion to action—and found me, he said, much improved. He built a lab in the house in Antwerp, where I, silent assistant, saw mercury in little spherical bodies running about, organs pickled in jars, leaves below a microscope. Over dinner the two men met and talked together, about Socrates, Descartes, the zodiac, free will, circulation, the poles. Why had they lost the Civil War? What was the way back to royal rule? Unlike Mr. Hobbes in his *Leviathan*, then under production in Paris, William thought that common man should be kept illiterate and happy, with sport and common prayer. "Too much reading," he said, "has made the mob defiant." I chewed my mutton and considered.

Too, we'd been making friends. There was Constantijn Huygens: statesman, poet, lutenist, and the translator of Donne into Dutch; the Duarte family, once Portuguese Jews, now merchants of coral, pearls, and diamonds (they had a Bruegel, a Titian, two Tintorettos); and Béatrix, Duchess of Lorraine, whose castle at Beersel was home to feminine sports of wit: lotteries, wishes, wonders, oracles. At first I merely listened at the duchess's gatherings, nibbled a butter cake. Yet in time I found I excelled at their aristocratic games. I wrote "portraits" for the ladies' amusement, riddles and allegories for them to untangle: the mind is a garden, married life a stew. To my growing delight, I was a hit, my mind, I wrote, a "swarm of bees." That August I cast off my years of mourning, sent maids scurrying down the halls with stacks of black gowns in their arms. To the final parties of the season I wore a rainbow of new dresses I'd had made—one as bright as a fiery beam, one as green as leaves. "After all," I told my husband, "dressing is the poetry of women." He heartily agreed. Had I heard it somewhere? I couldn't say. I took to wearing feathered hats like ladies in the streets.

One night, the Duarte girl sang poems set to music in a voice so clear I felt my soul rise up inside my ear. In a garden of clematis, with servants dressed like Gypsies placing candles in the trees, we assembled on the grass, between a Belgian wood and Béatrix's glassy pond. In a pale orange gown I read two pieces I'd prepared:

Queen Elizabeth was declared the radiant mistress of the sea, but Penelope should have been stalwart, I said, and never allowed those suitors to gather around her at all. When the ladies clapped their approval in the dark, everything, to me, was suddenly bright and near.

As autumn came, however, I found myself less often at Beersel, less often with William under the roses, more in my chamber alone. I filled sheet after sheet in my straggling hand—no one knew what with. And when he inquired at breakfast one morning: "I've long found pleasure in writing," I explained, "but was only joining letter to letter and word to word. Now," I said, and took a bite of pear, "I begin to connect idea to idea, as the ancients would form pictures of the stars." William suggested that a writer requires an acquaintance with the world, some external stimulation. "Might not a brain work of itself," I countered, "as a silkworm spins out of its own bowels?" I would benefit, he maintained, from engagement outside the house.

And the roses wilted and fell. The yard grew brown, then gray. Christmas came with its myrtle crowns and almond marchpane and candles. The ink in my inkpot was frozen every day. When John Evelyn, Lady Browne's son-in-law, came on a visit through Antwerp, he brought news that Descartes had died. An era had ended, the men agreed, or another just begun. That night, over supper, they discussed their old friend's work. The table was heavy with flowers and food, the fire was hot at my back. He was a man who knew much, the gentlemen agreed, and knew what to do with all that he knew. He thought the soul was attached to the human body through a gland, I remembered. He thought the universe was like a machine, the body like a clock. He'd once nailed his wife's poodle to a board. He believed nothing could think or feel but man. But how could he know a poodle didn't feel? Or even a magnet? A vase? Now he was gone, and I ate my bread. And yet, I thought, he lived. Unlike my sister and mother, Descartes was here, and always would be, as Shakespeare would, as Ovid. But I did not feel like a clock, I thought. I listened. I chewed my bread.

Then the Scheldt froze and William finally insisted I get out, spin on the ice with incorporeal legs. Much to his astonishment, I refused to do as he bid. Nervous, thrilled, I paced my chamber bit by bit, worried, as I wrote, that "should I Dance or Run, or Walk apace, I should Dance my Thoughts out of Measure, Run my Fancys out of Breath." I suppose he thought I wrote new riddles for the ladies at Beersel. I pondered in secret the link of death to fame: "Give me a fame that with the world may last." Yet also: "Fame is but a word, an emptee sound." I wrote: "And though it seem to be natur'l, that generaly all Women are weaker than Men; yet shurly some are far wiser than some Men." Still, the river would not thaw. At dinner one night Mr. Evelyn reported seeing a crow's feet frozen to its prey. I stared at him as if confused by what he'd said. I wrote: "Some Ground, though it be Barren by Nature . . ." and fish froze unmoving in the Scheldt. Sitting close to the fire one night, I burned the hem of a dress, white lace curled black upon the tiles. I wrote: "Some Ground, though it be Barren by Nature . . ." and stamped the flames with a moldy copy of Dodoens's *Historie of Plants in Antwerp*. I wrote: "Some Ground, though it be Barren by Nature, yet, being well muck'd and well manur'd . . ." Then Antwerp was flooded by melting ice. I wrote: "Some Ground, though it be Barren by Nature, yet, being well muck'd and well manur'd . . ." Peasants filled the city. Cows floated off. Birds sang. Fish swam. I wrote: "Some Ground, though it be Barren by Nature, yet, being well muck'd and well manur'd, may bear plentifull Crops, and sprout forth divers sorts of Flowers."

I wrote.

LONDON

1651–1652

SINCE A WOMAN WAS, IN THE EYES OF PARLIAMENT, A MINOR NO
matter her age, and since there could be no use in having children
swear a loyalty oath, now women swept into the courts as never
before—an Olivia for her Endymion, an Alice for her Ralph—and
it occurred to William, still in Antwerp, that this might be our
chance. He had been banished, yes, but a Royalist's wife was free
to return. So when Sir Charles began to plan a trip to London, William decided that I would go as well, and ask that I be awarded my
share of his assets. "That the time is right I have no doubt," he came
to my room and said. Yet for me, for the life of my mind, his timing
could not have been worse. Everything excited me—the nature of
flattery, food, poetry, the nature of shyness and wit—and I'd been
writing every day as in a rush it tumbled out. Now all this I locked
away in the tortoiseshell cabinet, fastening its tiny key to a chain
around my wrist.

No storms, no pirates. Just a dreary trip with many fraudulent fees.

By the time we reached the Thames, Charles was out of cash and had to pawn his clock-watch to proceed to the city upstream. We took a modest house in Covent Garden. From its narrow windows we watched the city stretching out: ticking, constant, grinding, chiming. Charles had early business with the Committee for Compounding. My own hearing would take place in several weeks.

First, however, I had my stepdaughters to meet. I'd carried gifts from Antwerp—black Dutch lace and clove-scented gloves—but Elizabeth and Jane were wary. London tittered. *Lady Cavendish went walking with ribbons round her arms!* Shy to speak in public, that much was clear, yet I did my utmost, so they wrote to their father, to stand out in a crowd. And *no one* wore feathers in London, yet their stepmother saw fit to be well-plumed when she went out.

Meanwhile, their father, their hero, whom they longed for, stuck in Flanders—too great a traitor to return. Too great a traitor, or so Parliament determined, to be given back any of the estates that had been taken. "And you were not even married when he fled. So technically," the judges ruled, "none of it is yours." I sat rigid before the court—my green, blue, red feathers drafting overhead. Unable to petition further, I whisperingly asked to be taken from the room, through the stately carved doors, out of Goldsmith's Hall to Gresham Street in December.

AT NIGHT I BECAME INCREASINGLY ANXIOUS, READING AGAIN IN A high-backed chair letters and poems William dispatched from Antwerp. Tales of virgins raped and flung from cliffs, bloody deaths for valiant princes, axes. Without me, he wrote, he was "cold as congealed ice," his tears "converted to a shower of hail." Each morning I walked to Drury House to inquire after his seized estates—meadows, coal mines, waterworks, granges—out of my control, sold to Parliamentarian officers. Nothing was as it should have been and London was grown strange. St. Martin's-in-the-Field was just plain Martin's. The House of Lords had been abolished. A new flag flew. Divorce was made legal. There was no aristocracy to set a sparkle to the city. The theaters were closed, the palace. Then one Wednesday even the sun went dark, and a burning halo replaced it. A preacher in Friday Street claimed the city's birds were struck dumb in the unnatural dusk, a mark of evil to come, and placed the blame on Cromwell's daughter, who refused the

Puritan cap, paraded in bright satin dresses. Gone were the jeweled vest and periwig. Men wore short-cropped hair and plain black suits and called each other "brother." Women in filthy skirts preached from London's corners. The underground Royalist paper, *Mercurius Pragmaticus*, declared England had "grown perfectly new, and we in another world." Time was "running up like parchment on fire." Change was "running up like parchment on fire." London was "running up like parchment on fire." I tried to stitch a pillowcase but found it deadly dull.

AS IF GOSSIP, INSOMNIA, AND PURITANS WEREN'T ENOUGH, DIRE NEWS
arrived from Antwerp. William had run out of credit again, and
this time there'd be no repayment from the queen. So Sir Charles
began the ignoble business of buying back his brother's inherited
estates, the rents from which would allow William a modest but
steady income. William's sons assisted. His daughters pawned jew-
elry and plate. And this new flurry of business meant another six
months in town. After six already? I sunk down fairly low. I reread
my husband's poems, their rivers of blood and wounded beasts,
and was troubled at night by dreams. In the mornings I would not
dress, since he for whom I dressed myself was miles from where I
was kept. I complained of headaches, constipation. Then one afternoon, three weeks on, Mayerne, the royal doctor, who'd often discussed me in letters with William, appeared in Covent Garden to
attend me in the flesh.

He tapped and patted, then scribbled in a book: how clear, how pale, how pink. I looked, he assured me, ten years younger than my age, in blossom, in perfect health, and prescribed only a new herb from China called tea. "The decoction of it drunk warm doth marvels," he told Charles. "Very comforting, abates fumes." To me he spoke nonsense, as he would to any child, suggesting candy or gossip, or candy with gossip, to lift my mood.

Sir Charles, meanwhile, had never seemed more engaged. Each night the house he'd let was filled with London's leading minds. There was the furor surrounding *Leviathan*, as Mr. Hobbes was back in town; some new map of the moon to decipher; and Thomas Browne, whose *Pseudodoxia Epidemica* was selling out across the land, busy addressing vulgar questions—such as whether the savior laughed—busy explaining time itself, and barrenness in women, and the reason so many aqueducts are adorned with a lion's head. All this I knew in some detail, for I admit I had grown curious, as days passed into weeks, and had begun to spend my evenings in a yellow parlor downstairs, listening as their voices pressed through the rented walls.

They spoke of Lucretius. They spoke of light.

One evening I took down *The Parliament of Bees* and, flipping through its pages, hearing the men enter the house, I counted seven years. It was seven years since I first sat listening to their talk . . . and I was as invisible this evening as I'd ever been in Paris. More so, in fact, for I sat dumbly and alone! Can you hide and yet be angry when no one looks at you? Oh, you can, I knew, but it was pointless, exhausting. The watchman shouted nine o'clock. Still their voices carried on. And despite the frost on the window, my cheeks began to burn—I thought I might be sick—so shrugging off my shawl, I hastened across the parlor and, throwing open the door, ran smack into Hobbes in the hall. "Dear," he said backing

up, "Lady Cavendish." He bowed as best he could. To which performance I said something dull about cabbage, something vague
about a bad fricassee I'd eaten, and hurried with a candle upstairs.

Once in my room, however, I felt foolish rather than ill. *I'm*,
I thought—and turned to the window—*I am much too*—and up
came a roar of laughter from the men. My face shone in the glass,
pale and round. A depressing little street: sleety, slippery, with
brash market voices, stinking heaps of trash. I could just make out
the edge of Bedford Gardens—then the moon broke free of the
clouds. London was transformed. London was set alight. The river,
the frost. Like something out of a dream. Like something out of
Shakespeare: hot ice and wondrous strange snow . . .

At last, all was silent, as if the house itself had froze. Yet even as
the river slowed and the city changed to ice, something in me loos-
ened, my thoughts were taking flight, into and out of questions I'd
long held, over London's rooftops, to the country, to converse with
an oak tree, a parrot, a clap of thunder:

Why do men deny fairies, yet burn witches at the stake?

Do fishes have brains?

Are stars made of fiery jelly or are they flecks off the sun?

That night I wrote: "I *Language* want, to dresse my *Fancies* in."

The following day:

> *Give me the free and noble style,*
> *Which seems uncurb'd, though it be wild.*

Hadn't I thoughts, after all? A mind of my own? It cannot be
infamy, I reasoned, to run or seek after glory, to love perfection,
desire praise. There were other ladies in London who wrote—I'd
met them at the secret Royalist concerts we'd attended. Yet the
poems they circulated among themselves were anonymous elegies

for dead children or praise for noble husbands. My own quill went marching across the page. I rejected any clocklike vision of the world. I chastised men who hunt for sport. The moon might be a ball of water, I proposed, and the lunar mountains we *think* we see only reflections of our own.

"Of Aiery Atomes."

"On a Melting Beauty."

"Similizing Thoughts."

"Thoughts," I wrote, "as a Pen do write upon the Braine."

I drew a glittering fairy realm at the center of the earth, its singing gnats and colored lamps. I would not leave the house.

Rumors swirled. Servants talk, of course. The floorboards creaked as I paced and spoke alone. The hallway went sharp with the scent of burning ink. Did I cook up incantations? They sounded half afraid. Pacing, yes, reciting my favorite lines. My mind was elsewhere, halfway to the moon. If atoms are so small, why not worlds inside our own? A world inside a peach pit? Inside a ball of snow? And so I conjured one inside a lady's earring, where seasons pass, and life and death, without the lady's hearing.

Of course, there were moments I faltered, fell suddenly into doubt. I'd never been taught, after all, and knew so little the rules of grammar. I'd embarrass myself, the family. I warmed my hands before the fire. Took up a fork and put it down. A woman on the street sang bleak hymns on the corner. Yet why must grammar be like a prison for the mind? Might not language be as a closet full of gowns? Of a generally similar cut, with a hole for the head and neck to pass, but filled with difference and a variety of trimmings so that we don't grow bored?

Then I took it a step too far: I would put forth.

THOUGH THERE WAS SCANTY PRECEDENT FOR WHAT I WAS ABOUT TO do, I hurriedly packed my papers and set out to St. Paul's churchyard, to the foremost publisher in England: Martin & Allestyre, at the Sign of the Bell.

An oddity from an odd marchioness? They snapped it up.

It would be public. It was done. I'd breathed no word to William and bade the publishers hold their tongue. I'd return to Antwerp shortly. I would rather seek pardon there than ask permission first.

LONDON TO ANTWERP

1653–1656

ONE WOMAN WROTE TO HER FIANCÉ IN LONDON: "IF YOU MEET WITH *Poems & Fancies*, send it me; they say 'tis ten times more extravagant than her dress." Then a week later followed that note with another: "You need not send me my Lady's book at all, for I have seen it, and am satisfied that there are many soberer people in Bedlam." But oddity is fodder for talk, and my book was soon required reading in London's most fashionable parlors. "Passionitt," they sniggered—it seems my spelling did astonish—"sattisfackson," "descouersce" for "discourse," even "Quine" for "Queen." Happily, I was already aboard a fourth-rate frigate bound for Antwerp. I saw a double rainbow, a porpoise in the waves. And when I arrived back home? William was astonished, yes, but not in the way I'd feared. He was proud. Far from being angry over the cost the printing incurred, he took it upon himself to send copies to his many and illustrious acquaintances. "It is a favor few husbands would grant their wives," I said, relieved, and this was true. Then the tidal wave of gossip arrived in the mail.

I set down a letter from William's daughter Jane. "It is against nature for a woman to spell right," I bristled. William only kissed my cheek. "Such ill-informed, seditious readers," he calmly said, "should exist beneath a marchioness's notice."

January, February, March.

One anonymous critic claimed that when he read *Poems & Fancies* his stomach began to rise—for Jane saw fit to send each notice the book incurred. Some readers were cross a lady had published at all, others that she had written of vacuums and war, rather than poems of love. William ignored the talk. He fenced and rode horses when the fashion was pall-mall. Still, I felt rotten, felt low. I hid and wished, or nearly wished, I had not published at all. I completely avoided the cabinet where my earlier writings lay. The days were short and dull, the garden in its thaw. Antwerp's blue-gray cobblestones went slick with rain and moss.

At last a mild evening: we took our supper outside, the leaves still off the branches, the stars so clear in the sky. Over pigeon pie and cherry compote, we spoke of his new horse. When I set aside my fork, William produced a note. "A letter has come from Huygens," he said, "who's been traveling in the south." He turned a page and read: "It is a wonderful book, whose extravagant atoms kept me from sleeping last night." The blood whirred inside my head. "What's this?" I managed to say. Here was a letter from Huygens—who mattered!—Huygens, who'd read my book. I could hardly hear the rest as William read aloud: something, something, something, vibrating strings, my book!

Thus by the time the spotted tulips blossomed, the nastiness of London seemed far across the sea. Indeed, it was a lovely spring. The sky was in the pond, the larks above. I tried to name each of the flowers we saw: double violet, lily, double black violet, plum.

William left Antwerp for a hunting trip in the Hoogstraten.

I, at last, unlocked the cabinet in my room.

THERE LAY EVERYTHING I'D WRITTEN BEFORE BEING SENT TO London: essays, puzzles, anecdotes, rhymes. Did I expect a trove of gems? I found some worthy ideas, but no structure to the mess. Still, it had to work—it must!—for there is more pleasure in making than mending, I thought, and I named it after an olio, a spicy Spanish stew (a pinch of this, dash of that, onions, pumpkin, cabbage, beef), sitting to pen a defensive preface: "This is to let you know, that I know, my Book is neither wise, witty, nor methodical, but various and extravagant, for I have not tyed myself to any one Opinion, for sometimes one Opinion crosses another; and in so doing, I do as most several Writers do; onely they contradict one and another, and I contradict, or rather please my self, since it is said there is *nothing truly known*."

Reading it back, I realized I believed it.

I was busy with two new pieces when a letter arrived in the mail: in the rented house in London, Sir Charles was stricken by ague. A week later, dear Charles was dead. William, just returned from the hunt, fell suddenly ill at the shock.

I split my days, so split myself: it was mornings with my husband, afternoons at my desk. My thoughts spun round, like fireworks, or rather stars, set thick upon the brain. Truly I mourned Charles, yet every afternoon I lit up like a torch. In one essay I called the Parliamentarians demons. Gold mines, I argued, could *not* be formed by the sun. My fingernails went black from the scraping of my quill. Few friends came to the house. Had I lost what friends we'd made? It was one thing to write riddles for ladies, another to do what I'd done.

Still, the summer invitations would arrive . . .

And so: at a soiree at the Duartes' I sat in black between Mr. Duarte and a visitor from Rome. I'd come alone—William too ill to attend—and grew sleepy on French wine as the two men spoke Italian across my chest all night. Finally, over boiled berry pudding, the Duartes announced a surprise: their eldest girl was pregnant, the pretty one who'd sung like a bird, now resting with her hands across her belly in a chair. Everyone raised a glass. I raised a glass. I looked around me, sipped the wine. To many healthy babies, I agreed. Yet I sank down into a private wordless rage, the fury of which I could not explain. I ordered the carriage, returned to the house. When William asked how the evening had gone, I snapped. Surely I had no time for such silly affectation. Only my work and my sick husband mattered. Nor was it easy labor. How many pages a day? How many days? Until, in the first fine week of autumn, as the branches in the orchard bent and wasps went mad with fruit, I set aside my quill. I'd finished my second book.

It was Michaelmas and William was recovered.

Now I myself fell ill.

William wrote to Mayerne that I was bilious, passed a great amount of urine with specks of white crystals in it. The doctor wrote back: "Her ladyship's occupation in writing of books is absolutely bad for health!" And what if it truly was? But if anything, I insisted, I'd only just begun, was off, at last, and thirty-one. I might be praised, I might be censured, but my desire was such, I explained, it was such . . . but I could not find the words. Judiciously, steadily, William worked to get me out—from my bed, my room, the house—and for his sake, I rallied. I promised him I'd lead a more sensible life.

Of course, by this time my manuscript was already off to London.

So one night, returning from a circus—monsters, camels, baboons, a man with sticks for fingers, a woman with soft brown fur—we opened the door to *The World's Olio* arrived in the publisher's crates.

WHILE ONE BOOK IN THE WORLD MIGHT BE CONSIDERED AN anomaly, two books, it seemed, sounded an alarm. The lady is a fraud! Even if the books were *ridiculous*, how could a woman speak the language of philosophy *at all*? I hadn't attended university. They knew I didn't read Latin. It fell to reason a man was behind my work—writing it, dictating it, or even perhaps unknowingly the victim of my theft.

But hadn't Shakespeare written with natural ability?

Every tree a teacher, every bird?

Alone in my room, I fought with the air: "If any thinks my book so well wrote as that I had not the wit to do it, truly I am glad for my wit's sake!"

DEFENDING A SECOND BOOK QUICKLY LED TO A THIRD. *PHILOSOPH-*
ical and Physical Opinions, 1655. In it I argued all matter can think:
a woman, a river, a bird. There is no creature or part of nature
without innate sense and reason, I wrote, for observe the way a
crystal spreads, or how a flower makes way for its seed. I shared
each page with William, often before the ink had dried. It put me
at odds, he explained, with the prevailing thought of the day. But
how could the world be wound up like a clock? It was pulsing, con-
tracting, attracting, and generating infinite forms of knowledge.
Nor could man's be supreme. For how could there be any supreme
knowledge in such an animate system? One critic called the book
a "vile performance." But another said my writing proved the mind
is without a sex!

At dinner parties now, I was sometimes asked to account for
myself, to speak of my ideas. I very rarely could. Bold on the page, in
life I was only Margaret.

Still, Antwerp, the parties, my husband's talks—all of it fed my mind. I'd hardly set down my quill before I took it up again, writing stories unconnected—of a pimp, a virgin, a rogue—strung up like pearls on a thread. This one, my fourth, called *Natures Pictures*, was something of a hit. It opens with a scene of family life—men blowing noses, humble women in rustling skirts—and closes somewhat less humbly, I admit, with "A True Relation of My Birth, Breeding, and Life"—in which, for the sake of history, I describe in my own words my childhood in Essex, my experiences of war, my marriage and disposition—in short, my life—and ultimately declare: "I am very ambitious, yet 'tis neither for Beauty, Wit, Titles, Wealth or Power, but as they are steps to raise me to Fames Tower." O minor victory! O small delight! My star began to rise.

ANTWERP

1657

I PAUSED IN THE HALL BEFORE GOING IN TO EAT. "I'VE HAD IT," William spat, "with this damned unending war." I took a spoonful of chestnut soup. "Yes," I said, and watched him as he chewed. He finished his dinner in silence, hulked off to his room. Alone with the duck and a vase of roses, was I to blame for his mood? The latest round of gossip had rattled him, I knew. "Here's the crime," he'd said in a fit, "a lady writes it, and to entrench so much upon the male prerogative is not to be forgiven!" He'd defended me at every turn. Yet lately he'd been riled. And for my part—riled, too—I decided simply to busy myself with the summer as best I could.

There was a housekeeper to hire.

A neighbor starting an archery school on the opposite side of our fence.

A portrait to sit for—or rather, I stood.

And Christina, Queen of Sweden, was on a European tour.

Of course I'd heard the stories, impossible to avoid: how the queen drew crowds in Frankfurt and Paris, where one lady, shocked, wrote that her "voice and actions are altogether masculine," noted her "masculine haughty mien," and bemoaned a lack of "that modesty which is so becoming, and indeed necessary, in our sex." She wore breeches, doublets, even men's shoes. She smoked. She'd sacked Prague. She wore a short periwig over her own flaxen braids, and a black cap, which she swept off her head whenever a lady approached. Most importantly, she'd be traveling to Antwerp next, and Béatrix in her castle would host a masquerade.

A Gypsy, a flame, a sea nymph? I wondered what to be.

Late one night, with the ball still weeks away, a messenger banged on our door. Voices from the courtyard, footsteps down the hall—I found William in the parlor and a letter on the floor. The Viscount of Mansfield, Charles Cavendish, Charlie, his eldest, was dead. A "palsy" was how the letter writer put it: raised a glass to his lips and choked on the lamb. "Inconceivable," William choked. He muttered to himself. Only thirty-three and alive last week. I reached out for his hand. Was there anything he needed? But he didn't see that the fire smoked. He didn't hear me leave. I stepped into the courtyard, where out under the whirling stars I prayed for a grandson, many grandsons, *legions* of grandsons for William, who sat in front of the fire with the blankest of looks on his face. I watched him through the windowpane as through a room of glass. Later, too—tossing, restless—I watched as if from another world as he sweated through his sheets. He took a glass of brandy. He drifted off at last.

Next came a flurry of letters, back and forth. William grew suspicious, suspected the widow—of what? And Henry, so long a second son, was quick to claim his dead brother's title, even as his sisters begged him to delay, ensure that Charlie's widow wasn't pregnant with an heir. William shouted at servants. He fired the cook, rang the bell. Meanwhile, feeling so far from my husband's grieving, I felt strangely aware of myself. My face in the mirror was only one year older than Charlie's had been last week. How odd that I could still feel like a girl, be made to feel it, feel the cold floors of St. John's Green beneath my feet—"Picky Peg," my brothers called me—yet my neck was beginning to sag, the skin grown soft and loose. I was all discontent. Angry, in fact. At Charlie for dying so suddenly, at Henry for causing William to suffer, at William for letting his children upset him as much as they did.

A week passed with hardly a word in the house.

I worked at poems, he on his book about *manège*.

At last, one night, he asked me to sit up with him, and I agreed to a small glass of wine. We settled on a sofa near the fire. A quiet rain was falling. A dog in the corner scratched. My husband began to cry. "Now my best hope is that his widow will be pregnant." He choked back a sob. "A link to poor Charlie," he sighed. He took out a handkerchief, blew his nose: "Of course, I do not blame you." I put down the glass of wine. "Blame me for what?" I asked. He fiddled with a ring. "I will never hold our disappointment against you," he finally said. His words, though softly spoken, meant, I saw, he did.

So, a carrying on of patterns: in and out of rooms, watching windows, imperceptibly closing doors. When the night of Béatrix's party arrived, William was dressed as a captain. I emerged from the marble staircase in layers of gauze and yellow silk. "A beehive?" he asked, and offered me his arm.

Birds still chirped in branches. The night was warm, bright with moonlight and the lanterns off carriages that lined the gravel drive. Once inside the castle, William wandered left, I right, glancing through rooms, over tables lit by tulips, and out the windows to stars. In elaborate gilded bird-beak masks, partygoers passed me.

Even the music was like a dream, a foreign, pulsing air. And there, in the bustling courtyard, I spotted her at last—Christina, Queen of Sweden. She was dressed as an Amazon. Her entire breasts were bared, her knees. O excellent scandal! O clever ladies' chatter! But privately I admired the queen's gold helmet and cape, and her hand that rested lightly on the hilt of her handsome sword.

The following morning, a messenger rang the bell. William was out atop a horse, so I received the note. The widow was not pregnant. I asked the cook to fix his favorite meal. Over a pie of eels and oysters, I gently broke the news. "It will all be for the best," I said. I didn't say it might be best for the widow as well. I didn't say: There's no telling a child will be any comfort to its mother at all.

WHEN THE SCHELDT FROZE THIS TIME, I STOOD AT THE WINDOW, watching Antwerp's well-to-do slide by. Their sleighs, gliding, were lit by footmen with torches. William easily persuaded me to go out. Bundled in blankets, we rode to the shore, to revelers skating, vendors selling cakes and fried potatoes under lamps. The frozen expanse glistened in the dark, icicles licking the pier like devil's tongues. William stepped down and waited for me to follow. And—oh!—how I longed to go, to dance with him on incorporeal legs. But I couldn't. Or I wouldn't. He climbed back up. We turned around. William looked strangely heartbroken, and we rode through the streets in silence. Then alone at my desk, I imagined a frozen river in me: "a smooth glassy ice, whereupon my thoughts are sliding."

ANTWERP TO THE CHANNEL

1658–1660

WHEN YOUNG KING CHARLES II CAME FROM PARIS TO VISIT HIS
brothers (the dukes) and sister (now Princess of Orange), William
proposed a ball: "Opulent, of course, yet fittingly refined." We
stuffed Delft bowls with winter roses—their petals tissue-thin—
and draped the painter's studio in silk. Dancing was of the English
country style, with arched arms and curtsies, embroidered twists
and knots. "Lavish," it was whispered. And sixteen hired servants
carried dinner on eight enormous silver chargers—half through the
eastern door, half through the west, meeting at a table in the center
of the room. I managed the evening from a confluence of my own,
a merging of myself, my present and my past, as if half of myself
were here, myself, while the other half was still in Oxford clutching
the queen's fox train. Back then I'd been but a maid—and awkward
and shy—whereas tonight I was a marchioness and seated beside
the king. "Did you know," he leaned in close, "you are something of

a celebrity in London?" In truth, I'd heard as much. Still, I blushed as pink as the ham. "And it seems your husband's credit," he winked, "can procure better meat than my own." At two in the morning, we toasted the Commonwealth's downfall. And seven months later, by God's blessing, Cromwell was dead.

WILLIAM WAS HUNTING IN THE HOOGSTRATEN WHEN THE NEWS hit. In Paris, Rotterdam, Calais, Antwerp, exiles danced in the street.

Cromwell was dead.

I was at my desk.

Then, a creeping kind of peace. For some months nothing happened. There were skirmishes, flare-ups, but nothing of any substance. Not until December of the following year was William confident of a speedy restoration. He began, in delight, to compile a book of counsel, to be handed to the young king at some sympathetic moment. "Monopolies must be abolished," he wrote. "Acorns should be planted throughout the land." But above all else—and here he was firm—the king must circulate, must be as a god in splendor, and make the people love him "in fear and trembling love," as they once loved Queen Elizabeth, for "of a Sunday when she opened the window the people would cry, 'Oh Lord, I saw her hand, I saw her hand.'"

He could not wait to be home.

But what could home mean now? To what did we return? Through my open bedroom window came the sounds of morning: the clip-clop of a horse's hooves, the steady hum of bees. I'd lived in exile half my life, in marriage nearly as long. There was the familiar wooden gate, the leafy garden path. Once, it's true, I'd wished the war would end, so we could live at Welbeck, where I knew William longed to be. The children in their beds, I'd thought, peacocks on the lawn. But the war had never ended, or it had not ended for us. I'd long ago stopped waiting for home to come.

Still, the king's words were never far from my mind. A celebrity, he'd said.

Now William finished his book of counsel and had it bound in silk.

I ordered two new gowns: one white and triumphant like a lighthouse, one bruised like autumn fruit.

FIREWORKS, SPEECHES, GUN SALUTES, A BALL. IN APRIL OF 1660, THE
Hague celebrated with King Charles II. William rushed to his
side. He hoped to be named Master of the Horse, but his reception was cool, the little book went unmentioned, and that post of
honor was granted to a handsome new courtier named Monck.
Snubbed—even as Marmaduke was made a baron, Lord Jermyn
an earl—William refused an invitation to join the king's brother
on the crossing, hired an old rotten frigate, and left alone the
following day. He never returned to Antwerp. He sent a letter
instructing me to remain where I was, a pawn for all his debts.
His trip took an endless week—they were becalmed in the middle
of the passage—but when finally he saw the smoke and spires of
London, his anger passed to joy. He said: "Surely, I have been sixteen years asleep."

ALONE IN MY ROOM, I WAS WRITING PLAYS. THEY WERE ALL-FEMALE plays for an all-female troupe. Of course, it was absurd. Women so rarely acted in public. Of course, I never meant them to be staged. "They will be acted," I said to no one, "only on the page, only in the mind. My modest closet plays." I smiled. I dipped my quill in ink.

The housekeeper knocked and held out a note. I took up William's instructions from the ornate pewter tray.

No more to be done, yet everything to do.

Flemish tapestries, drawing tables, lenses, the telescopes from Paris, books, of course, and perfumes, platters, ewers, ruffs, tinctures, copperplates, saddles, wax. There were little green-patterned moths dashing around the attic, bumping at the glass. I thought I felt like that. I dreamed the moths crept upside down on the surface of my mind. In the mornings I met with a magistrate or bid a neighbor farewell. I myself packed linen-wrapped manuscripts into crates. The plays had a box to share, each handwritten folio tied with purple ribbon: in *Bell in Campo*, the Kingdom of Restoration and the Kingdom of Faction prepare to go to war, and the wives, with Lady Victoria at their helm, insist on joining the battle; in *The Matrimonial Trouble*, a housemaid who has married the master proceeds to put on airs; in *The Convent of Pleasure*—the only not quite finished—Lady Happy, besieged by men who wish to marry her fortune, escapes to a cloister. But the pesky men sneak in, dressed like women, to join the ladies' play within the walls. Enter Monsieur Take-pleasure and his Man Dick.

Monsieur Take-pleasure. Dick, Am I fine to day?

Dick. Yes, Sir, as fine as Feathers, Ribbons, Gold, and Silver can make you.

Takepl. Dost thou think I shall get the Lady *Happy*?

Dick. Not if it be her fortune to continue under that name.

Takepl. Why?

Dick. Because if she Marry your Worship she must change her Name; for the Wife takes the Name of her Husband, and quits her own.

Takepl. Faith, *Dick*, if I had her wealth I should be *Happy*.

Dick. It would be according as your Worship would use it; but, on my conscience, you would be more happy with the Ladies Wealth, than the Lady would be with your Worship.

Takepl. Why should you think so?

Dick. Because Women never think themselves happy in Marriage.

Takepl. You are mistaken; for Women never think themselves happy until they be married.

Dick. The truth is, Sir, that Women are always unhappy in their thoughts, both before and after Marriage; for, before Marriage they think themselves unhappy for want of a Husband; and after they are Married, they think themselves unhappy for having a Husband.

Takepl. Indeed Womens thoughts are restless.

Then scenes change according to my whim, for I was writing more freely than ever before. In the cloister one moment, we're next on a field of green, where sheep graze around a maypole, and Lady Happy is a shepherdess, while the Prince-who-woos-her-as-a-Princess is a shepherd. Next, Lady Happy is a Sea-Goddess and the Prince-as-Princess is Neptune astride a rock. They embrace, as friends, and then as friends they kiss. Happy questions her fate. Truth be told, she felt a certain stirring. And "why," she asks, "may not I love a Woman with the same affection I could a Man?" In the end, the Prince's true nature is revealed. But would Happy, who fled all men, be happy to be his? I hadn't yet decided, but hurriedly placed a lid atop the crate, then marched myself and my household to the shore. The goods and lower servants boarded a frigate. I, at last, a Dutch man-of-war.

THE RESTORATION

IT CAME AS A SHOCK. AFTER A BRUTAL CROSSING—IN WHICH SHE HIT her head in a storm and swore she'd seen a bear at the helm of the ship—Margaret expected to find her husband at his London residence, Newcastle House, in fashionable Clerkenwell. Yet there she stood in Bow Street in a rented house, again. "I cannot call it unhandsome," she said when asked if she liked her new room. Where was she meant to keep her gowns? It hadn't even a mirror. William's steward came to tell them that her crates could not be found. Her sister, Margaret learned, would be in Cornwall for three weeks. All this in the first two hours, still stinking of the ship. A doctor came, declared her sound. Margaret washed. She slept. In morning light, she dressed. And over the following week, as William prepared to petition the courts for the return of his elegant townhouse, Margaret prepared for some sign of the notice she'd allowed herself to expect.

A celebrity, the king had said.

She sat by the window day after day, yet no one they knew would be walking in Bow Street, and no one in Bow Street seemed to notice who she was.

This was the Restoration, after all. The very air in London was filled with triumphant returns. When the king arrived on his ship in the Thames, twenty thousand horse-and-foot stood brandishing their swords. Everyone had their version of events. Everyone spoke at once. John Evelyn, from the Strand, beheld it and blessed God: "Praised be forever the Lord of Heaven, who only does wondrous things." "A pox on all kings!" cried a hag. "Oh look, the king," gasped a girl held aloft. The diarist Samuel Pepys wrote of bonfires the city over, an infinite shooting of guns, and men drinking to the king's health upon their knees in the street. London was born anew, again. The theaters reopened in a glow of candles and laughter. There were public lectures at Gresham College—on astronomy, on wind. Throngs of visitors, exotic ambassadors. There was tennis at Hampton Court.

Amid this tumult, Margaret's crates went undelivered. Her manuscripts were missing. She had only two gowns on hand.

"Did you know," she said over toast one morning, setting aside a letter from her sister, "it is the fashion in London for a lady to appear in public in a state of near-undress?"

"Ah," said William, and grabbed his hat.

He had always some appointment or some old friend to see.

"My dear," he sometimes offered, "if you wish to come, then say."

But Margaret said nothing, or hesitated, and William left, annoyed. When he returned in the evening, he'd find her seated alone at the table in one of those two gowns.

"Are you feeling well?" he'd ask.

"Yes, My Lord," she'd say.

She tried to write, but nothing came.

"My dear," he said one evening, "I believe we must do more. We were gone so long, you see. We must work to make ourselves known in London's good society. After sixteen years stalled, we must finally begin to act."

His wife looked past him to his shadow on the wall.

"Margaret?" he asked. He scraped his fork against his plate: gingerbread and apple cream.

"But I was not stalled," she said.

When her sister returned from the country, Margaret was summoned for cake. In rose silk shoes she ventured out, saw that Bow Street teemed with rats and worse: narrow, rutted, splattered by offal and urine, the houses pitched precariously overhead. She saw a painted whore in a gilded chair. A dead dog on the corner. Then Catherine rattled on about people Margaret hardly knew. "How relieved you must be to be home!" her sister cried. "But why are you staying in Bow Street?" And Margaret tried to explain: their debts were large, the estates tied up. They must wait for the king to restore some fraction of what they had lost.

"You've a smudge on your face," William said when she got back.

Margaret touched her nose.

"Other side," he told her.

At least when he attended the lectures he'd report on what he'd seen: a demonstration on falling bodies, something pretty with mercury, a piece of white marble dyed a most dramatic red. And though women were not allowed at Gresham College—Cromwell might be dead, but not everything had changed—Margaret waited and listened. For every hour, it seemed, an exiled thinker returned, while others were back in the city after years in university towns.

Soon William's interest was especially piqued—so, in turn, was hers—by a group of experimental philosophers who'd met at Oxford during the war. The Invisible College, they'd called themselves, within the college walls.

"Invisible?" she asked.

"A network, you know. Sending letters, sharing ideas."

He stopped to pinch some salt.

"In any case," he said, "despite the war, whether Royalist or Roundhead, they spent hours together in John Wilkins's garden, testing ideas. It's all about proof, you see."

"Remind me, who is Wilkins?"

"You remember. That preacher who wrote the book about a colony on the moon."

Together they chewed the goose.

"In addition to ivies," William continued, "this garden boasted a transparent beehive from which the men extorted honey without disturbing the bees . . . a rainbow-maker misting exquisite colors across the lawn . . . a Way-wiser and Thermo-meter . . . and a hollow statue with a tube in its throat through which Mr. Wilkins could travel his voice and surprise any guests to his garden!"

"How merry it sounds."

William nodded, spit fat. "Productive, too."

Now scores of pamphlets were being printed each day—flicking down London's streets, catching horses' legs—and all of it in English—not French, not German, not Latin—so that Margaret could, for the very first time, read the new ideas herself when they were truly new. There was one on fevers, one on flora, one on a frog's lung, one on fog. At first there were words she did not know and explanations she could not fathom. But as days passed into weeks, she saw a pattern emerge: one man referred to another's research in explaining his own findings; one article led you down a path of thinking to the next. And there was one pamphlet in particular causing quite a stir: *New experiments physico-mechanicall, touching the spring of the air* by an Irishman from that Invisible College, a man named Robert Boyle, currently blazing to fame though wholly unknown to her. Margaret sent a servant to fetch it from a shop. In its pages she learned of years of careful labor: the construction, at Oxford, of an air pump, and the subsequent experiments performed on living things.

Prior to the lark, she read, Boyle used a mouse.

The time before, a sparrow.

Before that, a butterfly.

And once he used a bee.

The lark, though now with a hole in her wing, looked lively enough when Boyle put her under glass. Then he turned a stopcock on his rarefying machine and the air was slowly sucked out of the chamber. The bird began "manifestly to droop." It staggered, collapsing, gasping. It threw itself down, threw itself down, and then the bird was dead.

"All this," she objected, "to prove a bird needs air?"

"Before devising the pump," said William, "he'd had to strangle them with his hands."

Now all London was buzzing with the news: air holds a vital quintessence necessary to life.

"Too late for the lark," Margaret said.

And as for the air, it was foul. London was loud and it stank. The streets bulged with noisome trade: salt-makers, brewers, soap-boilers, glue-makers, fishmongers, chandlers, slaughterhouses, tanners, and dyers hemorrhaging rainbows into the rivers and lanes. The windows were dimmed with sooty grime. At night she couldn't sleep. She panicked in the dark. Was it wrong to miss her blue-domed room and the orchard back in Antwerp? It rained, and

Margaret slept all day. She dreamt that a porpoise swam up to her window and gulped. Why couldn't she find a handkerchief? Where was her summer coat? She would send her plays to Martin & Allestyre, but her crates still had not arrived. "Where are my crates?" she asked the maid. Where were her linen-wrapped plays? Her mind was like a river overspilling in the rain. Robert Boyle, Robert Boyle, currently blazing to fame. So William called a doctor, who bled her into bowls. Her cheeks were red, then pink, then gray; the blood in the bowls was black. That night another storm blew in and hit upon the glass. Still the sounds of London's bells came clanging in her ears: St. Martin-in-the-Field, St. Dunstan-in-the-West. One, two, three, four . . .

By dawn, the sky was clear.

"Where are my crates?" she asked, now calm.

And William proposed a ride, for she'd been so long shut in. But London Bridge was adorned in traitor's limbs set at startling angles. She saw a leg splash into the river. A rat ran down their hall. The watchman bellowed, "Rain!" No one knocked on their door.

At last, one night, Margaret insisted that they go—retreat to the countryside, where she could write and be at peace. She had never been happy in London, not once. "And to be surrounded by such a constant crush, all of them speaking English!"

"But you never learned a word of Dutch."

"Exactly," Margaret countered. "I cannot distinguish my thoughts!"

"My dear," William finally said, "Welbeck is uninhabitable. Bolsover is half pulled down—six rooms in the eastern wing stand open to the sky. For that matter," he dug in, "your St. John's Green is nothing but rubble and hip-high grass."

She told him of her sister's disdain for their lodgings, of that rat she had spied in their hall. It was an insult, she half whispered, to live so far below their rank. Was this what they'd suffered for? Her childhood home flattened; one brother crushed by his horse; another shot in the head. So that they might return, unnoticed, to live in Bow Street in filth? She trembled as she said it: "Unfit, it appears, to be acknowledged by the king?"

William only chewed his meat. He wiped his lips. Then he pushed back from the table, loyal to the crown. "To my final breath!" he cried.

Days of silence settled with London's soot on the house.

But the following week, when a grocer's boy was trampled to death just beyond their doorstep, William acquiesced, moved them over to Dorset House just up from the Whitefriars Stairs. It was only one elegant wing rented from the earl, and though he could ill afford it, William had to admit: the move brought quiet, and river views, and an ample parlor with an Italianate ceiling in which to entertain.

SIR KENELM DIGBY, SIR GEORGE BERKELEY, THE BISHOP OF LONDON
himself: Margaret greeted them in the Dorset House parlor in
a dress of sparkling violet, a hat like petals falling through empty
space. To William, so pleased with it all—the guests and wine,
her sparkling gown—his wife was more a marchioness than she'd
ever been before. He remembered her in Paris, pretending to read
or sew. Now as he took her round the room—introducing her to
poets, ambassadors, dukes—she hardly blushed, and even spoke.
Yet meanwhile, across the parlor, his daughters looked on dis-
traught. Their father had grown only more besotted and their stepmother more astonishing than when they'd first laid eyes on her in
ribbons years before. She bowed. She nodded. She nearly bobbled.
Yet if she noticed their scrutiny, Margaret gave no outward sign.
She admired Elizabeth's sapphire stockings with the metal thread.
Elizabeth smiled sweetly. Everyone played a part.

Finally, one quiet morning, word arrived at Dorset House that the king would come to dine. It was exactly what William had been angling for these weeks. He hurried to write a spoof—the evening's entertainment, involving an incomprehensible Welshman who babbles when meeting the king—while Margaret was taken down to see the Earl of Dorset's cook. Quince cream and orange pudding, the harried cook advised. Quince cream and orange pudding, singers and a band. The morning passed in a fuss. A hasty dinner, and rain began to fall. Margaret, exhausted, alone in her chamber, sat and watched the barges on the Thames: onions going down to sea, timber coming up. She had not written in many weeks. The river raced along. A fishmonger dropped a basket and several fish slid out.

William hoped for a place at court, his London house returned, and Margaret had hopes of her own that night. "A celebrity," the king had said.

As guests began to arrive downstairs, she was thinking her thoughts, half dressed.

"What is it?" William asked as they descended the marble stairs.

She only shook her head.

The parlor was overfull: ladies grooming, musicians tuning, powder on the air. Here came her one living brother, John, whom Margaret hardly knew. William's son Henry. Sir Kenelm Digby, again. Guests danced, drank punch. They threw open windows for air. But when the king's carriage was seen in the street, everything grew still. Margaret stood beside her husband, the blood loud in her ears.

His Majesty entered to fanfare—and all was movement again.

William was first to step forth and bow. The king turned to Margaret, who smiled and curtsied low. It was their first meeting in over a year, their first since that dinner in Antwerp, yet when she opened her mouth to speak, she saw the king's eyes riffle over her and off. Over her shoulder he scanned the crowd. On instinct, she moved aside.

He was lost all night to a sea of girls and courtiers and fuss. Quince cream and orange pudding, singers and a band. At least William was named a Gentleman of the Bedchamber, at last.

"An utter success," her stepdaughters confided to Margaret as they prepared to take their leave. "The handsome king! That spoof!" Still the rain persisted, and the bishop had lost his hat. Maids danced in and out. Where was the bishop's hat? Alone at the window, Margaret didn't hear. The reflection of the parlor was yellow and warm. She watched it empty out. Then, an interruption. A voice came at her side: "What do you look at with such interest, Lady Cavendish?" What did she see in the glass? She saw the Marchioness of Newcastle. She saw the aging wife of an aged marquess, without even any children to dignify her life.

THE VOICE WAS RICHARD FLECKNOE'S AND HE SAVED HER FROM HER-self. "We've met before," he said, "at the Duchess of Lorraine's . . . at Béatrix's castle." By now the parlor was empty and he stooped to kiss her hand. The king was gone. The parlor was empty. Flecknoe was kissing her hand.

He began to visit daily. He knew her work and praised it to her face. Dramatist and poet, and newly returned from Brazil, he was the tallest man she'd seen outside a circus. He wore a black stiletto beard, dressed head-to-toe in black.

"Your devotee?" asked William.

"Do you think he's a rogue?" Margaret asked.

· Yet he seemed so fresh, so young, even if not, in truth, so many years younger than she. And the strangest expressions fell from his mouth: "All my cake will be doe."

They began to go on outings; William approved, amused.

One morning Flecknoe took Margaret to see an amaryllis. It was grown in a pot by a gentleman named Fox. There were many witty young people around, some claiming to have read her books. And what did she think of the flower? "Like two lilies lashed at their feet," she said. She declared it somewhat mannish. Her audience approved. "Look, you are a star," Flecknoe whispered into her hat.

Another afternoon, as he perched like a crow on an Ottoman stool, Margaret asked her new friend to describe the vast Atlantic. "Oh, it was most abundant," he said, putting down his glass. He told her of the savages. Of garish birds and waterfalls and Brazilian rivers and death. He hoped to visit Greenland next. "I shall take you to see Mercator's map!" he said, on display in a mansion near Whitehall.

The following morning they walked the Strand, past cab stands and Roman baths and the stalls at Covent Garden. All was renovation, the king importing new styles from France—the long dark wigs and silverwork doublets, aviaries and fountains and gardens shaped like stars—and Flecknoe bent low to tell her how the previous night the king's brother had secretly married Anne Hyde. "The court is in a state!" he laughed.

The map was under glass.

Annotated in Latin, she could see for herself that the northern tip of Scotland—*Scotia*—crept onto its bottom edge. At center were four islands: one green, two yellow, one pink, which, he told her, comprised the North Pole, a whole divided by four indrawing rivers to a whirlpool in the middle. "Here," he said, "lies the very pole of the pole of the Earth, where all the oceans' waters circle round and fall, just as if you'd poured them down a funnel in your head, only to see them come back out the southern end. And in the middle of the middle sits a large black rock, the very pole of the pole of the pole of the Earth, wholly magnetic, possibly magic, and thirty-three miles across!"

"Where is the ice?" she wanted to know.

Walking back up the Strand, he explained about floes. But rather than return to Dorset House, he proposed they venture on—from Fleet Street to Ludgate Hill, up Friday Street to Cheapside—to a coffeehouse called Turk's Head in Cornhill.

"Have you never been, Lady Cavendish?" he asked.

"Please call me Margaret," she answered.

It was dim inside, yet most heads lifted when Flecknoe stooped in with a marchioness on his arm. He placed her at a table with several of his friends—a James, a Henry, a Gibson, a Joseph, a Balthy, a Cutch—then returned with coffee, gritty and sweet in a dish. She thanked him and sipped as his friends resumed their conversation about the London stage. A stack of dirty dishes mounted as they spoke: of Beaumont and Fletcher, Ben Jonson's *Volpone*, of Davenant's new wings. When the talk turned to a technicality of narration, Margaret abruptly spoke. "Have you noticed," she said, "how few plays begin or end with a woman's character speaking?" The one called Gibson readily agreed. But Margaret said no more, and soon it was time to go.

That night she only poked at her food. Her stomach turned. In bed under a canopy—a dusky swath of red—she was struck just after midnight by the vision of a gown—a dress for the North Pole!—the first she'd dreamt up in ages. And very early, in a kind of violent compulsion, too eager to wait for her husband's consent, she sent off an order for three bolts of bright blue silk, and gilt lace, and green and yellow taffeta . . . but how would she manage a magnetic hat?

Then, of a sudden, William was ready to leave London.

It wasn't Flecknoe's recent request for patronage, or the money she'd spent on the gown. He'd simply come to face his fate: he would never find a position in the king's innermost circle—too old, too stuffy, a reminder of the past.

Margaret said she was ready, if readier months before.

"Wasn't this what you wanted?" he asked.

"It was," she said. "It is."

"What is it you want, my dear?"

But Margaret wanted the whole house to move three feet to the left. It was indescribable what she wanted. She was restless. She wanted to work. She wanted to be thirty people. She wanted to wear a cap of pearls and a coat of bright blue diamonds. To live as nature does, in many ages, in many brains.

"I want my crates" was all she said.

The following morning, before she'd even risen, William was off to Whitehall Palace to seek the king's permission to leave. If he couldn't hold sway at court, at least he'd be lord of his county, as he had been before the war, the most powerful man for over half a million acres—from Kegworth to Three Shire Oak and all the way back around.

NOTTINGHAM WAS A NOT INCONSIDERABLE TOWN, WITH WIDE streets and sturdy houses, shops of salt-glazed pots, and Wensleydale and Cheshire cheeses, and stockings and licorice and ale. They stopped at the inn overnight. Morning brought the forest. Sunlight shot from spots between the trees, a dizzying reiteration as the carriage rushed along. It was the farthest north she'd ever been on the planet. The land seemed wilder to Margaret than anything she'd seen. William saw something different. He reminisced. Where once had been the densest of woods, branches entangled like fingers in a grasp, now stood a modern and managed park: timber for building, charcoal, hunting for the rich. Yet to her eyes, Sherwood Forest was vast. It was thick with green and black with moss and lit by starry mountain-laurel clusters puffed up in the dark.

They stopped to stretch.

Margaret heard a heron's plaintive *franck*. There were mushrooms on rotted bark, cinnamon ferns in mud. So here was England, yet again—not London, that calamity—England. But it might as well have been the moon, so alien to her memories, to gold soft fields and hills. "What is that?" she asked, head cocked to the side, and he answered it was a river, hidden in the brush. It sounded unlike any she'd ever known. Not the Scheldt, nor the Thames or Seine. "Does every river make a music of its own?" she wondered, tired. Thames, Trent, Tees, Tyne, Tweed, Tay, Dee, Spey: names of rivers, south to north, she'd memorized as a girl. "Margaret," he called from the carriage, for it was time to go—but something rustled, something whistled, something rattled, remote or close. Thames, Trent, Tees, Tyne, Tweed, Tay, Dee, Spey. Of course, this forest was famously enchanted, enchanting, and heavy with its fame. Her feet began to sink. "Margaret," he called from the carriage, "we're almost there."

WELBECK SPANNED CENTURIES: GOTHIC AT ONE END, ELIZABETHAN in the middle, and at the other end a classic Jacobean front. Inside, the house had been denuded in the war. Fortunately, Henry's wife—who'd lived there with her family until William and Margaret's return—left several beds, and pots and pans, and candlesticks and stools, and two imposing suits of armor erect on a red leather floor.

"Still, it's nice," William murmured, "to be at home at last."

For days he seemed ceaseless, sleepless: there were his nearly horseless stables and the crumbling castle of Bolsover not a day's ride to the west. His holdings spilled over borders, into Derbyshire and Yorkshire, and, riding through, he discovered many fewer deer, missing fences, and missing woods, yet was happier each night at supper than his wife had ever seen. He arranged with merchants for iron grates for their fires, glasses for tables, linens for beds, then met with tenants until midnight to settle disputes at The Swan. Margaret watched him come and go, Lord Lieutenant of Nottinghamshire. He could arrest a man, raise a tax, argue for hours about bullocks or plows. He appeared to her a stranger wearing her husband's skin.

She wandered from empty room to empty room, mapping the house with her feet, in gold shoes that echoed off the walls. It was a little, she decided, like living at the Louvre, so frigid and bewildering, though she'd never tell him that. From its formal entrance and polished stairs, the house pushed back from the London road, turned right and south to water gardens, left to the ancient monastery out of which the whole building had sprung. Her own vast chamber was on the second floor, puckered by a wall of oriel windows, each pane divided into sixteen squares that glittered in the dawn. A yellow writing table faced the southern wall. Hung with heavy tapestries, the bed looked like a ship. Against her will, it seemed, she fell asleep by day, the bed as dark as night, and when she woke, her dreaming filled the chamber. But Margaret detested a nap, the day flapping loose all around. She scribbled: "Idleness is the burden of my sex," but nothing else. She had nothing to do and no one to see—William off working, no rats in the hall, no Flecknoe to entertain her. She had nothing but time, and no reason not to write. Each hour that passed with no ink from her quill was a quiet affliction, a void. She stared at that sunny table, ill fitted to the room, and watched as a violent downpour passed over their lake and woods.

Soon Margaret took to sitting in a room a floor below her own, a medieval wood-paneled gallery painted like a rainbow the century before. It was here she came to read in the afternoons.

And there that William found her, one day, and invited her on a walk. It was a filmy winter afternoon, and he'd show her the path to Clipstone Park, his chosen boyhood province, just beyond their woods—past the ornamental canals, the fishpond, swans upon the lake. He took her hand as they rounded the water, a scene he had often described. But when they cleared the trees, he met instead with a shock: stump after stump after stump after stump after stump and dried-out shoots. He sat on the ground. The sky was white. The day was everywhere quiet. "I left it," he finally said, "so full of trees. And a river of fish and otter. And rabbits and partridge and poots." Now he grieved. Now everything hit him at once. All he'd lost was lost in that grove. "Sixteen years," he said. And Margaret helped him up. She took him home and sat him before the fire, placed a blanket over his knees—he was almost seventy, after all—then settled down beside him to watch the falling sleet. The clock chimed ten o'clock. "Damned Roundheads!" he cried at last. "Damned charcoal! Damned war!" That night they shared a bed, as once had been their custom.

Yet in the morning, out the window, in addition to the frost there was the grange farm that needed tending: cattle, oxen, horses, rye. He pulled on his boots in the icy hall. The winter was hard, and a new kind of normal settled with the snow. No one came to visit. No neighbors for miles around.

"For my pleasure and delight," she wrote in a letter to Flecknoe, "my ease and peace, I live a retir'd life, which is so pleasing to me as I would not change it for all the pleasures of the publick world, nay, not to be mistress of the world."

So passed several months.

She even tried to help with the sheep.

Then, one spring day, her missing crates arrived.

SHE WAS READING FRANCIS GODWIN'S *MAN IN THE MOONE*—ITS MAN borne into space in a carriage drawn by swans—when she heard the sound of wheels upon the gravel. Two boxes from Martin & Allestyre were set down on the drive. "My modest closet plays," she said. She nearly ran to the stairs—for the recovery of her wayward crates that spring and the preparation of her plays for publication had rekindled inside Margaret a flame she'd feared gone out. Indeed, she'd said to William: "a flame I'd feared gone out!" But now, in turning the pages, she grew concerned and then incensed: "reins" where she had written "veins," "exterior" when she had clearly meant "interior." The sun went down. The room grew dim. She tipped a wick into the fireplace and nearly lit herself—*ting ting ting* went the kitchen bell—then hurried with a candle down the long and flickering hall.

William was already seated before a small beer and lamb. Margaret placed a napkin in her lap.

"Before the printer ruined it," she cried, "my book was good!"

"Could it be," he asked, soaking his bread in blood, "that you were yourself the cause of this misfortune?"

"It could not," she said, and took a bite of pie.

"Perhaps," he said, "you had not yet come, at that time, to so fully understand the words which you were using. You've been on such a course of reading that I'm sure you will be happier with the next."

Cyrano de Bergerac, Francis Bacon, Robert Hooke. And pamphlets from that Invisible College now chartered and renamed: the Royal Society of London for the Improvement of Natural Knowledge, with rooms at Gresham College and a silver mace from the king.

"I suspect they gave it very little attention," she finally said. "A little book by a little woman, they thought."

That night she wrote to Flecknoe: "My wit at last run dry!" Since leaving Antwerp, since returning to England, she'd written nothing new, only tidied up those plays. "And yet," she pressed on, "perhaps these plays will find some profitable use?" She snuffed the candle, closed her eyes.

But weeks passed with no word from Flecknoe, no word about her book. The summer grew heavy with rain.

"Margaret," William asked one day, "what is it you are doing?"

"Revising my books," she said.

"I've long admired your books as they are."

"And that is a huge consolation to me," she told him, "in this censorious age," but went on fixing sour rhymes, replacing omissions, undoing misplacements—and not only words but entire passages, theories. "Now," she said, and dipped her quill in ink, "it will be for all history as if my errors never were."

"And you're happy in our new life?" he asked.

"Very happy, My Lord."

Again, he worked to get her out. They watched a licorice harvest near Worksop one day, where millions of capricious insects glittered in the fields. They shared a radish salad, spotted a white-tailed deer. And when they returned to Welbeck that night, a letter was waiting from William's daughter Jane.

Now Margaret learned that readers thought her plays lacked all direction: no catastrophes, no drama, just a jumble of speeches and scenes. They tire the brain. Only flit from place to place.

"But I'd have my plays," she said, still standing in her jacket, "be like the natural course of all things in the world. As some are newly born, when some are newly dead, so some of my scenes have no acquaintance to the others."

"Surely you cannot hope to please every reader, my dear."

"It seems I cannot hope to please a single one!"

And as the leaves yellowed, Margaret withdrew. The evenings grew darker faster. She sank into herself. William had seen it more than once, yet he couldn't always be there. He spent some nights each week at Bolsover Castle, attending to the rebuilding: an entire new roof for the western wing, where rooks had nested and frogs in puddles croaked. Ensconced in her rainbow gallery, Margaret sat late with pamphlets by Hooke, Boyle, and Wren: on optic lenses, windy holes, or ways of killing rattlesnakes, or making maps from wax. Then Christmas arrived. Then New Year's Eve with oysters. Her stepchildren paid a visit.

"Come, Margaret," William said.

"Come along," the grandchildren called.

At last, she stepped outside. She squinted in morning light. Small green shoots shot up across the yard. Spring had come to Welbeck in a burst of green-winged orchids. Margaret walked to the village in a hat like a Chinese fan. The villagers hadn't seen her in months, only heard of her from the household staff. An old man in the market square wore bluebirds on his arms. She passed the bakery, the dress-maker's, and then she opened a door. For she'd ordered a book—Francis Bacon's *New Atlantis*—and began to read it there in the shop, of a traveler caught in a storm, led to discover an unknown world, the utopian Bensalem, its Salomon's House the ideal college of learned men: investigating, experimenting, for the good of all mankind. "We must hound Nature in her wanderings," she read. Unlock her secrets and penetrate her holes. "Break her," Bacon argued, "and soon she will come when you call." The stationer watched the marchioness. As she read, her face grew taut. She closed the book and turned to go. He watched her cross the busy square toward the path back to Welbeck alone.

IT BROKE UPON HER WITH THE RAIN. AFTER NEARLY TWO YEARS OF stagnation, fearing her wit run dry, as the rains washed over the forest, muddying roads, and the bluebells bloomed, Margaret sat and wrote . . .

Orations of Divers Sorts, Accommodated to Divers Places is set in a nameless city somewhat like London, a little like Colchester, and a bit like Antwerp besides. This is how it starts: Margaret invites the reader to imagine herself in a market.

Imagine yourself in a market that bustles.

The sunny smell of hay and shit. See stalls of cabbage and leek, fish with frosted eyes, baskets of eels and flowers. See herbs and chickens, hanging capons, and soap and cows. See the barber who performs surgery on a man with bleeding teeth. See packets of peppercorns, dry-salted meat. There are musicians somewhere, tuning, and many men preparing to step up onto boxes and speak.

But all around you, too, observe the ruins of war. You have only to alter your gaze to witness endless rubble. Dress in comfortable shoes—we'll be moving from place to place—yet in something fit to be seen, for who knows if we'll happen upon the king playing tennis in the park. Have no fear, gentle reader, for you will be returned to your home, and safely, as soon as the orators have done. But expect disagreement, hullaballoo. Some men will argue for war and others for peace, some for the rights of the rich and others that all ownership is theft. Then, in the middle of the day, with the sun at its summery zenith, after a series of speeches that are none too kind to women, and despite the fact that women are not born orators, we women, who've been listening, will gather ourselves to speak.

The first of us will say: "Men are so Unconscionable and Cruel against us, as they Indeavor to Barr us of all Sorts or Kinds of Liberty, as not to Suffer us Freely to Associate amongst Our own Sex, but would fain Bury us in their Houses or Beds, as in a Grave; the truth is, we Live like Bats or Owls, Labour like Beasts, and Dye like Worms."

The second will add: "Our Words to Men are as Empty Sounds, our Sighs as Puffs of Wind."

The third counter: "We have more Reason to Murmur against Nature than against Men, who hath made Men more Ingenious, Witty, and Wise than Women, more Strong, Industrious, and Laborious than Women, for Women are Witless, and Strengthless, and Unprofitable Creatures, did they not Bear Children."

The fourth propose: "We should Imitate Men, so will our Bodies and Minds appear more Masculine, and our Power will Increase."

"Hermaphroditical!" the fifth will cry.

"Masculine Women ought to be Praised" will say the sixth.

And the last of us will speak: "Women have no Reason to Complain against Nature, or the God of Nature, for though the Gifts are not the Same they have given to Men, yet those Gifts they have given to Women are much Better."

In 1662 Margaret's *Orations* was published—to outrage, wonder, and scorn.

THE BLAZING WORLD

IT IS A COLD MORNING IN EARLY SPRING. THE SUN HAS RISEN; THE sky is piled with clouds. Soon the snow will fall. Over the trees, the pond. The cows and pigs and sheep. Now smoke rises from a chimney in the village, a grayish plume into the grayish sky. The little village houses are not visible from the window, not through the woods, the innumerable leaves, though on certain days, if the wind is right, she can hear the village children shouting and playing games. She can smell the bacon fried. When she drives through in her carriage, when she makes her daily tour, she sees their faces peering out from cottage doors. She is a specter. A spectacle? The snow will blanket the road.

Margaret stands inside her room and stares out at the grounds. It is early spring. Or is it winter's end? So much now is changed. Yet like the flakes beyond the window glass, some years rise up while others sink down, out of her view, without concern for order. She remembers a day six years ago, which feels much further back, how the fountains plashed with wine—soldiers, trumpets, a drift of pigs in the street. Every bell in London swung. It was the king's thirtieth birthday, and he arrived on a ship awash in satin and guns—the *Royal Charles* moaned in shallow water—then disembarked and spat upon the ground. "A pox on all kings!" cried a hag. He flipped on a wig and mounted his stallion, rode with billowing hair down billowing streets, the bluster of many horses' hooves muffled by petals and tapestries, puddles of wine and shit—Fleet Street to the Strand to Charing Cross to the palace—then ordered Cromwell's traitorous head severed from its body, stuck up on a twenty-foot spike above Westminster Hall evermore.

Or had she only heard that part from William?

She paces as it snows. Her skirts wave around her as she takes this morning exercise, fold upon fold of fabric unfurling in continued variation. Of course, it doesn't snow inside her room, onto the floor, the Turkey carpets, yet every other minute she flicks her hand before her face as if hurrying away a flake. No, winter is kept outside. Or is it early spring? In any case, the room is warm—stuffed with roses, a blazing fire, the honeyed air her husband finds so stifling. He prefers she visit him in his chamber a floor above, where the *Ballad of Robin Hood* is painted on the ceiling. He isn't at Welbeck today, however, gone to London on forest business, having been named at last the Justice-of-Eyre. Not the position he'd hoped for at court. At least they are a duke and duchess—she is Duchess of Newcastle now.

But I am old, she thinks, turning to the mirror.

She touches her hand to her neck.

Normally, she would begin her writing directly, but her newest book, really two books in one—*Observations Upon Experimental Philosophy and The Description of a New World, Called the Blazing World, Written by the Thrice Noble, Illustrious, and Excellent Princesse, the Duchess of Newcastle,* which she calls one part Fantastical and one part Philosophical, "joined as two Worlds at the end of their Poles," and in the preface of which she claims to be "as Ambitious as ever any of my Sex was, is, or can be; which makes, that though I cannot be *Henry* the Fifth, or *Charles* the Second, yet I endeavour to be *Margaret* the *First*"—has just returned from the printer.

She is anxious for its reception, plans to send a copy to the king, copies to Oxford and Cambridge. On her desk this new book sits, leather-bound, a strange and reverent object. It marries, Margaret thinks, all of my life's work. And she opens it at random to a passage near the start, finding the Emperor of the Blazing World leading the visiting Duchess of Newcastle to see his horse stables of gold, cornelian, amber, and turquoise—they are utterly unique!— whereupon the duchess confesses that "she would not be like others in any thing if it were possible; I endeavor," she tells him, "to be as singular as I can; for it argues but a mean Nature to imitate others; and though I do not love to be imitated if I can possibly avoid it; yet rather than imitate others, I should chuse to be imitated by others; for my nature is such, that I had rather appear worse in singularity, than better in the Mode." Surely it shines, she thinks. And she wishes it one thousand or ten thousand million readers. Nay, that their number be infinite! The Blazing World with its blazing sky and river of liquid crystal. Its gowns of alien star-stone! Its talking bears and spiders! William has told her it is her finest work, and even composed a poem to include:

> *You conquer death, in a perpetual life*
> *And make me famous too in such a wife.*

Margaret shuts the book.

Her eyes burn from reading too long by candle last night: one new pamphlet from the Royal Society called "Some Observations of the Effects of Touch and Friction" and another, well-thumbed, from Hooke's *Micrographia; or, Some Physiological Descriptions of Minute Bodies Made by Magnifying Glasses with Observations and Inquiries Thereupon*, on the discovery of a new world—not a *new* world, she thinks, for certainly one's inability to see something does not mean it is not there until one does—opened for the first time to his sight, with so-called new stars and new motions, and in particular one section regarding the moon, wherein Hooke, observing light near the Hipparchus crater, concludes that the moon "may have Vegetables analogus to our Grass, Shrubs and Trees; and most of these encompassing Hills as may be covered with a thin vegetable Coat, such as the short Sheep pasture which covers the Hills of Salisbury Plains," as well as the description of an experiment that may, he writes, reveal a hidden world beneath our very feet, beyond the reach of even the most powerful microscope, an alternate universe of harmony and vibration—and hadn't she thought the very thing herself, and years ago? A world inside a peach pit? Inside a lady's jewel? Yet he magnifies a flea to fill a folio page, as if to turn nature into a monstrosity is the most profound success. He turns a flea into a thing not wholly flea!

So it's for the best—it is, and she will not regret it—that in this new book she addresses these men directly. Of Hooke and his *Micrographia*: "The inspection of a bee through a microscope will bring him no more honey, nor the inspection of a grain more corn." She calls their microscopy a brittle art. Hooke himself admits it! How the light inside the instrument, coming from different angles, causes a single object to take on many shapes. They distort the very thing they claim to expose! Indeed, she pities the flea. Meanwhile, their so-called observations reveal only the outer shell, and nothing of the inner essence of a thing. The mysteries of nature go utterly unrevealed! She even challenges the Royal Society to debate her ideas in public, for why should it be a disgrace to any man to maintain his opinions against a woman? "After all," she says to the mirror, "I am a duchess and not unknown," and she straightens out her heavy skirts, twisted all around.

The light in the room is piercing. Now the clouds have gone, it pours in through tall windows, made harsh by the whiteness outside, echoes sharply off a collection of mirrored boxes and several glass drops—a gift from her old friend Huygens, whose son has just completed his own new book, *Systema Saturniam*, in which the rings of Saturn are described—so she calls her maid, Lucy, to pull tight the heavy drapes.

"It was a mighty storm, Duchess," Lucy says as she pulls.

"No letters today?" Margaret asks, still waiting for word from William.

"Not today, Duchess. Though Mr. Tapp says the London road is down with snow. You'll likelier hear tomorrow."

Lucy curtsies, closes the door.

Alone again in semidarkness, Margaret stands in the corner and fancies herself a statue, with silken robes and a crown of topaz, erected in a garden, atop a pedestal, at the center of a circle divided into four parts, with lines drawn, and points laid, in the service of some abstruse mathematical thought, and covers her eyes with her palms. She can see her Blazing World before her: the emperor's bed is made of diamonds. The walls of his room are jet. His penis is made of silver. She opens her eyes. No, it's just a penis. But there are his horse stables of gold, cornelian, amber, and turquoise. There are his horses. This is his golden city, his flickering canal, his woodsy archipelago stretching all the way to the granite cave where Bear-men sleep on the cool dirt floor. She imagines the salty musk. She imagines the cave steaming, drenched, covered in moss and crystals.

The binding cracks. She sniffs it. Her book smells like a shoe.

Then, as if she's been struck by alien star-stone, she's suddenly struck by doubt. Is it ridiculous? Is she a joke? Not that these doubts are new, only here, again, and racing in the dark. And where moments ago she saw a golden city, now there is only this. The fallen snow. This dread. She places the book in a shallow drawer, scans the room to fill her eyes and so to fill her mind: the bed, the mirrors, the tapestries, a portrait of herself. But even with the curtains drawn she finds her eyes are burning, a headache coming fast, and she calls again to Lucy to assist her in retiring to a sofa of pillows embroidered with garden scenes. Off come her skirts and petticoats, her lace cuffs and collar, her shoes and whalebone stay, until she lies on her side in nothing but a cotton shift and endless strands of pearls. Dust hangs in a crack of light between red velvet drapes, like stars.

Her dreams are glimpses, bewildered—celestial charts, oceanic swells, massive, moving bodies of water, the heavens as heavenly liquid, familiar whirlpools, the universe as a ship lost at sea—but the ship she imagines arrived safely, years ago, loaded with their possessions. It's true her crates took long to find her—something mismarked or misnamed—and she wept for her missing manuscripts as she would have wept for an absent child. Long reconciled to childlessness, she worries instead about barrenness of the brain: "I should have been much Afflicted and accounted the Loss of my Twenty Plays, as the Loss of Twenty Lives," she's written, "but howsoever their *Paper Bodies* are Consumed, like as the Roman Emperours, in Funeral Flames, I cannot say, an Eagle Flies out of them, or that they Turn into a *Blazing* Star, although they make a great *Blazing* Light when they Burn"—and as she wakes, her mind alights on something she read last night, Copernicus's dying words: "It moves!"

*

When he returns, the snow is melted, the almond trees in bloom. "I nearly forgot what you looked like," Margaret says. It was only those two weeks he'd planned for, plus another six or seven he could never have foreseen.

William has brought her a gift: *Experimental History of Cold*, the latest from Robert Boyle, which includes an account of experiments touching the force of freezing water, experiments touching the weight of bodies frozen and unfrozen, bodies capable of freezing other bodies, and bubbles formed in ice. "It is," he says, "the latest talk of learned men."

She turns it in her hand.

Like throwing an apple into the pond without causing a single ripple—has no one read her *Blazing World*?

"Give it time," says William. The plague has only just passed, if it has; the theaters are still black; the birdmen with their leather masks still step between the corpses. Yet when he praises Boyle's book, Margaret gets tart and raspish; she can feel it, and dislikes it, and she walks a path through the garden thinking *Margaret Margaret Margaret*. I am old, she thinks. I am ugly. "But you do it again and again," he has said. "Into what depths of despair had you let yourself fall before receiving those letters from Flecknoe and Hobbes in praise of your plays?"

"Give it time," he says.

So Margaret gives it time, and William gives Margaret a pony: black with a star on its crown.

Together they ride to Creswell Crags, where cool wind whistles in and out of caves, and spiderwebs like watery nets link the tallest branches. Head tipped back, she asks: "Might not the air be made like that? Little lines, clear and close, which stretch across the universe and hold us all in place?" William cannot hear; he's ridden ahead; she's alone with the wind and the spiders. Why else don't we float into the sky?

In a copper tub of lukewarm water scented with burnet, water mint, and thyme, Lucy colors Margaret's hair, with radish and privet, to give it back a reddish glow, for on Tuesday they'll be visited by John Evelyn and his wife, whom Margaret hasn't seen these many years.

"Not since Paris?"

"Not since Antwerp, at least."

They arrive, John and Mary, in a plain coach thick with dust, though Margaret, curtsying deeply, assures them that she's never seen one finer. Together they view the grounds—the alley of fir trees, the riding house, a black and trumpeting swan—and as they turn around the lake, William begins an account of a demonstration he witnessed in London, in which a spaniel and a mastiff were each tied to a table. "The spaniel was bled out one side," he explains, "while the blood of the mastiff was run into the spaniel through a quill." The mastiff died on the table. But the spaniel was taken to the country to recover. "Remarkable!" Evelyn says, sorry to have missed it. They fall behind to talk. Meanwhile, Margaret notes Mary is smartly dressed, in a long-waisted bodice, a narrow skirt draped and pinned in back. Her own shimmering sea-green dress billows like a wave.

"That a person might even think up such a thing," she says at last, as if in answer to a question.

"The dogs?" says Mary. "But surely you see that here is progress. Imagine the possibilities."

"No, my dear, imagine the risk. Such hubris."

They pass before the stables, which stink in summer heat.

"Nature," Margaret advises, "is far too vast for you or I to comprehend her."

Mary says nothing, still in her traveling hat.

Then Margaret tries again, for truly she once loved Mary's mother, Lady Browne, now as dead as her own. "Do you remember," Margaret smiles, "how you carried my bridal bouquet?"

Back in the house: a chilled silver bowl with ripe fruits from the garden. Lunch is lamb from the flock that munches the nearby hill, and stewed chicken with prunes, and boiled leeks, and salmon, though Margaret eats only a clear broth and clarified whey with honey, hoping tonight for success on the stool.

"You and your duchess are absolute farmers," Mary smiles at William, who credits a recent rain.

"Naturally," Margaret says, "every part and particle in nature hath an influence on each other, and effects have influence upon effects." But Mary only eats her lunch, while, over the raisin pie, Evelyn tells how plague deaths are down in nearly every parish. How Hooke established the rotation of Mars. How Hooke discovered tiny rooms called "cells." Of coming trouble with the Dutch. How a lead actor in Davenant's company killed a man in a duel in a play. And an invention the size of a pocket watch meant to slice a human foot into many thousands of parts.

"For whatever possible reason?" Margaret finally blurts.

"For mathematical purpose," says Evelyn.

Back outside they drink their wine. Blue and yellow flowers dot the garden wall. The couples split again: he with him and she with her. In gaps in his own conversation, William hears his wife: "I am sufficiently mistress of," then, "with the devastating clearness that I do." The sky is light as servants refill their glasses, yet evening shadows begin to creep cool air across the lawn. The two men soon fall quiet. "It is a great pleasure to me to write," Margaret is telling Mary, "and were I sure that nobody read my books, yet I would not quit my pastime."

"Indeed, Duchess," Evelyn says, turning in his chair, "I've heard admiration of your new book."

"Have you?" Margaret says—but jumps in her chair, for someone shoots in the woods.

"*The Discovery of a New World Called the Blazing World*," he says.

"There, you see," William says, taking a bite of fruit.

"From Samuel Pepys," says John, "who works in the Navy Office."

"Yes?" she says, straining to seem relaxed, as *pop! pop! pop!* go the woods.

"Indeed, he declares it quite romantic. Also from Robert Boyle, author of *The Sceptical Chymist*, you know, who," he turns to catch William's eye, "is lately writing an account of objects that oddly shine. Inspired, I am told, by a piece of rotten meat found glowing in his pantry."

William and Mary smile.

"Forgive me," John says, coming back to Margaret, "for I have not had the pleasure of reading your book myself."

But before she can ask him, *What were Boyle's words?* John has turned and attends his wife, who is speaking to William of their garden in Deptford, its many species of trees. "Conifers," Mary tallies, "and laurels, oaks, and elms." Margaret dabs her upper lip. Robert Boyle, she thinks. Robert Boyle. Samuel Pepys. She dabs her neck, her lip. She has had too much to drink. But would it be rude, she wonders, *not* to acquaint him with my book? On such a pleasant night? For he says he has not read it. Yet Boyle has, she thinks, and a man called Samuel Pepys. She could easily fetch a copy. She could read them the passage about Descartes . . . or the description of the Bird-men . . . or the one about the microscope . . . or the vehicles made of air . . . "Two potted limes!" laughs Mary, and John and William smile. Still someone shoots in the nearby woods, and a flock of rooks rises from the treetops like a cloud.

In bed that night, she won't be sure what she said next. She'll remember how the cloud of birds rose up over the trees. It begins as in a dream, she might have said. Then the cloud broke up and found itself again. But thing must follow thing. She must put her thoughts in order. I pray, she might have said, that if any professors of learning and art should humble themselves to read it, or even any part of it, I pray they will consider my sex and breeding, and will fully excuse those faults which must unavoidably be found . . .

"It starts as in a dream," she likely said, "with the abduction of a lady, stolen by a merchant seaman, taken to his ship and into a mighty storm. Next comes the death of the merchant and his men. For after that storm, the ship drifts not only to the pole of the world, but even to the pole of another, which joins close to the first, so that this cold, having a double strength at the conjunction of two poles, is insupportable. Too weak to throw their bodies over, the lady lives for days amid blueing flesh, kept alive by the light of her beauty and the heat of her youth as the ship floats across the fish-bright sea. Eventually, she and the vessel pass—mysteriously, unavoidably—into the other world, a world called the Blazing World, where cometlike stars make nights as bright as days. When at last the lady spies land, it glitters with fallen snow, and talking bears, up on two legs, are coming to her rescue. But she is unable to eat what the gentle bears offer, so the bears take her to Fox-men, who take her to Geese-men, who take her to Satyrs, who take her to meet the emperor of the land. They travel for days on a golden ship in a river of liquid crystal."

Then darkness fell, and John and Mary rose, but Margaret wasn't tired. John and Mary curtsied, bowed. Margaret stayed and watched the moon wheel across the sky; she climbed the stairs; she lay upon the sheets.

Might it have been more prudent, she thinks, lying there in the room, to have better explained the book's more serious philosophical contemplation, for without it the other half no doubt sounds pure fancy and could be easily misunderstood? The night is hot and close. An owl calls in the woods. Margaret sleeps. And she dreams of that room without a mirror on Bow Street, and Robert Boyle asleep in the bed with her *Blazing World* on his lap, open to a passage about a golden hollow rock, which produces a medicinal gum, which causes a body to scab, which scab will open along the back and come off like a suit of armor.

"Some believe I act as if drunk," Margaret reports one night in early autumn, "as I stammer out words, or only pieces of the letters of words." "You're not so bad as that," William replies, dipping bread in soup. A letter has come from London with most distressing news. It seems Mary Evelyn—"Was Deptford near to the fire?" he asks, but how should Margaret know—that Mary Evelyn has reported to her vast London acquaintance how Margaret's "mien surpasses the imagination of the poets; her gracious bows, seasonable nods, courteous stretching out of her hands, twinkling of her eyes, and various gestures of approbation, show what may be expected from her discourse, which is as airy, empty, whimsical, and rambling as her books!" Evelyn himself, the letter writer maintains, came to Margaret's defense, arguing that in the duchess's body are housed together all the learned ladies of the age. "Never did I see a woman so full of herself," countered Mary, "so amazingly vain and ambitious." "Not that I should care what Mary Evelyn thinks," Margaret says, pushing away her plate. I have made a world, she thinks, for which nobody should blame me.

"Yet it's true I am so often out of countenance," she says, walking with William in the garden before bed, "as I not only pity myself, but others pity me, which is a condition I would not be in." Despite her radished curls and pleasant curtsies, Mary Evelyn has called her masculine and vain!

"My tongue runs fast and foolish," she despairs the next day at tea, "so much, and fast, as none can understand." In the sweet-smelling room, a pendulum clock: *ping, ping, ping, ping.* And looking across the table, she finds her husband grown old. No, only weary, she thinks, reaching for some toast. There have been so many disputes, and tenants unable to pay, and the draining of the marshes . . . "The truth is," William suddenly says, "women should never speak more than to ask rational questions, or to give a discreet answer to a question asked of them. They ought," he wipes his mouth, "to be sparing of speech, especially in company of men." To which surprising rejoinder Margaret sits in silence, her throat blocked up with bread.

The lady floats for days across a fish-bright sea. At least it isn't putrid; the cold contains the smell. In the galley she finds a crate of pears and eats one right after another, on the floor beside a frozen boy, listening to bits of ice bump against the hull. She is strangely unafraid. Hadn't she always longed for adventure, back at her father's home?

On the fifth night of this solitude, she falls asleep with a candle burning and dreams herself a mermaid with a thick and golden tail, a crown of shimmering conch shells, then awakens with a start. Whether the ship hit something or something hit the ship, another change has come. The ship is dying; she can feel it slipping away. She waits beneath the blanket for icy water to greet her. But instead of the sea, it's a bear that opens the door.

A great white bear up on its hind legs steps across the threshold.

"Good morning," he says, and reaches out a paw.

"Is it morning?" she says, and stands, though this belies her shock. For here is a talking bear! And she clicks through stories she's read or heard: seizing children in the night, yes, and claws and hunger. But, too, constellations. And in "East of the Sun and West of the Moon" the bear is a prince all along.

"We must hurry," says the bear.

"Certainly," she says. "Yes," she covers herself with her arms, "the ship is sinking," as though she's only just realized, the floor of the cabin now swirling with water and small silver fish that bump against her toes. Still, she does not move.

"Miss," he says, more urgently now. But she only stands and stares. So he takes her in his enormous arms and rushes to the deck. The water rises around them, and from her perch she sees the sun has also risen—or rises, still—and at last breaks through the clouds that have surrounded the ship for days. The ice, too, is breaking up in all directions. The sea is itself again. She sees bodies stiffly bobbing. But the water and sunlight have raised the bear's fur to a gleam. He is blinding: bright as snow in springtime. She shuts her eyes.

"Where are we going?" she shouts above the waves and another noise—a shrieking. Is it the ship itself that cries?

"There," he says. He pants.

She opens her eyes again to a rocky spit of beach, just beyond the prow. A dozen bears wave their paws at them and frown as if to say: *Hurry*, or *We don't think you're going to make it*, or *All this trouble for a girl?* A hole is opening, a sea-mouth fit to swallow them up. Is it the water, she wonders, that makes the terrible noise?

"Hold on tight," he shouts, so she holds him.

She rides him to the shore, where he lumbers up on all fours, then sets her down and shakes. Seawater rains over her (the bear is nine feet tall, at least), and several of the silver fish slide out of his fur and gasp. The other bears surround them. They seem impressed, or else amused. One of them helps her to her feet. They sniff her, not impolitely. She can hardly think to stand with all the shrieking. She glances up at the sky and sees massive circling parrots—it is they who make the noise! The beach is sharply pebbled. The lady wears no shoes. The bears give off a musky, fishy smell. One of them offers a blanket made of fur, but not of bear. Sailors' bodies dot the bay. She smells salt. She smells the musky bears, hears them softly discussing whether to pull the sailors to shore, whether or not to eat them. Yet, she is unafraid. If she shakes, she shakes now from the day, which she feels at last, her skin growing pale and blue in the insupportable cold.

"Come," says her rescuer, a warm paw on her back.

Behind her, the ship has disappeared.

"Silver, silver, silver!" a maid shouts in the hall, and Margaret can hardly believe it, for when was the last time she went anywhere at all? Now the whole house prepares for departure, and the servants are talking of spoons. One room swirls with feather dusters and motes of dust in light—they must be alive, she thinks, for see how they are nourished by the presence of the sun—and maids are throwing linen over chairs.

It's off to London now, for Newcastle House in Clerkenwall has finally been regained. Or has it been repurchased? In any case, it's William's. He is anxious to see it, be in it again. It was built, he tells her, on the ruins of a nunnery, in the Palladian style, with thirty-five chimneys and views in all directions. He asks her what she hopes to do in the city. It's been so long since she was there. The carriage bounces south. Toward Robert Hooke and Robert Boyle. Gresham College and public lectures. And that modest house Sir Charles rented in Covent Garden, where—so many years ago—she wrote her first book in a trance. "Shall you sit for a portrait?" William asks, but she hadn't thought of that.

Outside the carriage, England unrolls in reverse: first forest, then farmland, then softly rising downs. They stop at an inn. They stop beside a brook that's fast with spring. It all looks the same, she thinks, if a brighter shade of green, since the last time she traveled this road it had been the end of summer. Or was it early fall? The following day, the traffic begins to grow. She sees carts of flowers and cabbages trundle toward the city. The farms turn to villages, the villages to town. There are even crowds along the roadside, trying to get a glimpse—of him? of her? she isn't sure. William declares it right, pulls her back from the window: "You seem to forget we are now among the highest aristocrats in England. Let them watch the grandees pass."

At last the carriage stops.

All she can see is a wall.

She hears the horses panting, brushes a fly from her lap. As they sit together in the carriage warmth, her eyes begin to close. Scraps of vision from the past two days pass beneath her lids: the scattered trees and bluebells; the sun upon a hill; a small white house with a thick thatched roof and a dog who appeared above her head atop a garden wall. Her eyes are shut. She smiles. Is it happiness she feels? She is back in London, her *Blazing World* a triumph. It was just as William said. She had only to give it time. There was first that letter praising the sharpness of her wit. Then one about divine fury, enthusiasm, raptures. And in a single afternoon two letters came from Cambridge. The vice-chancellor called her an oracle. The Master of Fellows of Trinity College called her "Minerva and an Athens to herself." Yes, there were others who never responded to the gift of a copy she sent. Still, she thinks. The horses shuffle. She sleeps.

Then, with a clatter of gears, a gate is pulled open in the windowless façade, and they pass through to a courtyard, which leads to a reception hall, which leads to gardens behind. The walls enclose two acres, complete with an orchard ready to blossom and the ivied relics of the ancient cloister that formerly stood on the grounds. Margaret steps outside. She breathes the London air. But William calls to her, eager to lead the tour. Thus Margaret learns "Palladian" means "balance." There are two symmetrical wings of the house, one built for the husband, one for the husband's wife. Though when he had it built, of course, his wife was someone else. It's this lady's portrait, blue-eyed and yellow-haired, that hangs in Margaret's rooms.

Yet she is happy—is it happiness she feels?—as she places her things in the cupboards and drawers. Her quills, stockings, shoes. The room is dotted by porcelain figures. *Punctuated*, she thinks. She picks one up, puts it down. The former wife's collection? Then opens a window to London bells and that green-silk scent of spring. And she sees now, here in this room, how badly she'd needed to leave. Impossible to perceive at Welbeck what one perceives in town. Or to perceive in London what one perceives anywhere else in the world. The rain in Paris, for example. Or the color of the cobblestones that run along the Scheldt. Of course, she thinks, a body cannot be in two places at one time. Might a mind? But no, she thinks. For when a body changes location, it changes its mind as well. She looks to the mirror. Her hair is graying, but her eyes are wide and green. On how many millions of occasions has she observed her own reflection? Tonight she sees that girl in the carriage so many years ago, en route to join the queen. Yet how hard it is to point to a moment. To say: There, in that moment, I changed. That night on the road to Oxford she felt she was plunging into life. The horses ran through the starry dark. And today, too. She closes the window. Everything comes together. The air is wet and sweet, and tiny star-shaped flowers creep across the lawn. She almost laughs as she unpacks a pair of gloves. I will call on dear Catherine in the morning, she thinks, and moves to sit on the canopied bed as Lucy hangs her gowns.

They eat, undress, dress again, drive out into the city. The city is half black from the fire. Still, there is birdsong and laughter. Swine root in fishy water. Towers strain, bells peal. Someone cries for a girl called Doll Lane. The carriage takes a left. Then Charing Cross, then Wallingford House, then Royal Park and the new canal. At last they disembark and enter the Banqueting Hall together, William greeting familiar faces, Margaret in diamond earrings and a hat like a fox that froze. They've come to pay their respects to the king and his new queen—new, at least, to Margaret—and pass beneath enormous chandeliers, Margaret in a gown designed to look like the forest floor, like glittering yellow wood moss and starry wood anemone and deep-red Jew's-ear bloom. It has a train like a river—so long it must be carried by a maid—yet hitches up in front, so she might walk with ease. Gone are the golden shoes with gold shoe-roses, just flat boots laced to her knees. Into the king's reception chamber—dizzying carpets and glasses of wine half-drunk—where Margaret grandly bows, but there's little chance to speak. Someone takes her arm. While William is left to speak with the king, Margaret is stewarded to the queen's reception rooms, where Queen Catherine sits surrounded by her Spanish ladies and several snoring hounds. How unlike Henrietta Maria and the old court this new one is: this queen is pious, unpretty, and has miscarried four times. Margaret's curtsey is solemn. Solemnly, she offers the queen a copy of her book. The queen is cold. Her ladies cold. "Are those Spanish dogs?" Margaret asks. She is not invited to cards.

"I hate it here," she says, climbing back into the carriage.

"You're far too easily flustered," William says.

In heavy rain they pass Arundel House, where the Royal Society—he's just learned from Lord Brouncker—has been meeting since the streets near Gresham College were damaged in the fire.

"Are you listening?" he asks.

The city is black and glistens.

A simple rule, which she should have remembered. "The most preposterous sort of ceremony," she says. For only the woman of highest rank is allowed a female train-bearer, yet Margaret has just presented herself to the queen in a train so long her train-bearer still stood out in the hall.

"An error," William says. "I'll apologize to His Majesty myself. You are simply out of practice. It's been nearly seven years. No need to make a fuss. There's no need to be always getting so upset."

They turn up Chancery Lane.

"Take Brouncker's wife," he offers. "A very amiable girl. One always finds—"

"At dinner tomorrow," Margaret says, "I will be entirely pleasant, you will see. I will limit my conversation to three topics: rain, Chinese silks, and the stage."

But the following afternoon, William hears her telling their guests that if the schools do not retire Aristotle and read Margaret, Duchess of Newcastle, they do her wrong and deserve to be abolished.

She sits with Flecknoe amid the porcelain figures and sips her cooling tea. It's true she's being spoken of. "The general air," he fears, "is sympathy for the queen. For they say your slight was intended, and you must have seen her pitiful face, and surely you've heard . . ."

But Margaret's mind is like a ball of string. It's just the same, she thinks. Nothing ever changes. And outside, it is spring. The orchard is in blossom. She rises to the window, sees the blooms on trees like constellations, the bees like tiny voyagers between the orchard's many worlds.

". . . her miscarriages," he whispers.

"But I cannot be sweet Lady Brouncker!" she blurts.

Now Flecknoe is quiet, and Margaret is sorry, for he only means to help.

"I should not have come to London."

"Nonsense!" he cries. "We must simply present you anew. Give them something else to rattle about. *Une petite soirée*, perhaps? Here in Newcastle House?" He unfolds into the room. "Surely the duke will agree," he says. "Is the duke at home?"

But no, the duke is out.

At suppertime, he comes. "Where have you been?" Margaret asks. But William only suggests they take their supper outside. After a plate of beef and two glasses of beer, he finally smiles and speaks. "I have written a play," he says. She nearly drops her fork. "*The Humorous Lovers*," he tells her. But they always share their work. "Opening night is in nine days. At Lincoln's Inn Fields. At eight." It's to be staged anonymously, since now he is a duke. "You may order a new gown," he says. He is eager, she can see. He kisses her on the forehead and tells her, "Everyone will come."

She is worried there's something she left behind. She has her mask, her gown. The *femme forte*, she'd explained to the seamstress. And so the dress, like an Amazon's, is all simple drapes and folds. Now she crosses Fleet River, her head held very straight. The water flashes in ropes, in shapes. Under the shadow of chestnut trees she stops to adjust her mask. There are others also dressed and moving toward the theater. A black glass bead in the back of her mouth holds the mask in place. She has never worn a mask before. She tries not to gag on the bead.

I am gallant. I am bold. I am right on time, she thinks.

She climbs the wooden staircase, takes her place in the box. And like ripples in a summer pond, lines of faces slowly turn—from the gallery, the pit—she watches the ripple spread. William must be late, for beside her is an empty seat. Still more and more faces turn. Margaret spies his daughters, who sit in a box nearby. Jane and Elizabeth avert their eyes, but they are the only ones.

It's not simply that Margaret's reputation has grown—her dress is gold, her breasts bared, her nipples painted red.

The play begins, the lovers center stage. William sits. Everyone roars. The candles sputter and hiss. Yet Margaret is as much observed as anything on the stage. Scene, scene, intermission, scene. The actors take their bows. The audience files out—chattering into coffeehouses, up onto horses, north to Hampstead, west to Oxford, south to the river and on—but before Margaret can say a thing in all the noise, William has her elbow and is guiding her through the crowd.

"Congratulations!" she tells him once their carriage door is shut.

"No, no," he says, "congratulations to you."

The horses lurch ahead, crossing the Fleet in the dark.

"Is something amiss?" she asks, placing the mask in her lap.

The river oozes beneath them, a blacker sort of black.

"What could be wrong?"

The driver turns north onto John.

"Only tell me," he finally says, looking out into the night, "exactly who wears such a gown to an evening at the theater?"

"The *femme forte*," she explains, "a woman dressed in armor."

"Do you think you are Cleopatra?" he asks.

Margaret bristles. She fingers the mask. "I had rather appear worse in singularity," she says, "than better in the mode."

"Do not quote to me from your books," he snaps.

The driver flicks his whip.

Margaret says nothing. She replaces the mask. The black bead rattles her teeth. Yet despite her continuing silence, she does see what she's done, sees it clearly, but from way down in, as if there is another mask she wears beneath the mask that she has on. She is a monster, she thinks, and hateful, after everything he's done.

*

Flecknoe arrives in the morning before she's finished her broth.

There's no question at all she wrote the play, everyone agrees.

"You are all that anyone talks about," he says. He offers the papers as proof. "Everywhere one goes it's only *Margaret Margaret Margaret!*"

She rings the bell for Lucy, but William has gone out.

And though her nipples are likened more to the nipples of London whores than any ancient heroines, that very afternoon the king comes to visit her. The king in her rooms. "A celebrity," he says, or said. Everything happens so fast!

"What are these daily papers?" Margaret says to William that night. "When did they begin?"

William is silent; he chews his fish; he takes a sip of wine.

"According to them, you wrote my play."

"I can hardly believe it," she says. And despite her feelings of regret, she cannot help but smile. Surely he sees the joke. "After all those years they claimed you as the author of what I wrote . . ."

"Tomorrow," William says, "they will be on to something else."

But tomorrow they are not. Each day for days the papers print details of whatever she did the day before: what floating restaurant she visited, her dinner guests, her gowns.

On April 12 the Duchess of Newcastle went out in a hat like a flame.

On April 18 she was visited by Anne Hyde.

When John and Mary Evelyn arrive, what choice does she have but to pretend that they are friends? Then Walter Charleton, Bishop Morley, many more. Soon her suite is full. William isn't there: he's at the palace, or the theater, or resting in his room. She's alone with the crowd and the porcelain figures. So Margaret recites: whole poems, theories, whatever springs to mind. She stands in the midst of her elegant rooms in the most fantastic dress:

> *If foure Atomes a World can make, then see,*
> *What severall Worlds might in an Eare-ring bee.*
> *For Millions of these Atomes may bee in*
> *The Head of one small, little, single Pin.*
> *And if thus small, then Ladies well may weare*
> *A World of Worlds, as Pendants in each Eare.*

On April 24 the Duchess has her brother, Sir John Lucas, to midday meal.

On April 29 she wears a hat like a little rose.

"You are a marvel," Flecknoe tells her.

But Margaret isn't sure. It's not as if she doesn't see what happens, doesn't watch guests turning away, especially some of the ladies, who cover their mouths with their fans. When Lucy comes to prepare her for bed, Margaret does not speak. She tries not to think at all—of the dinner parties, the afternoons, her shallow tinselly speeches—cringing to remember the transparency of her talk. And when she wakes the following morning to small red dots sprung up around her mouth, she sends Lucy to the apothecary's shop for velvet patches in the shapes of stars and moons.

"These black stars serve," she says to William, "like well-placed commas, to punctuate my face."

"They look obscene," he says.

On May 1 the duchess goes out in her silver carriage.

On May 2 she walks the lawn in a moiré gown.

And Flecknoe tells her—as they walk that lawn—how the previous night he heard someone telling someone else that after visiting at Newcastle House Mary Evelyn told Roger Bohun that women were not meant to be authors or censure the learned—he lifts a low-hanging branch—but to tend the children's education, observe the husband's commands, assist the sick, relieve the poor. Everything is white, for the blossoms have come down. The path is white. The grass. Even Margaret's shawl is white and wrapped around her arms. Eventually, she says: "A woman cannot strive to make known her wit without losing her reputation." "But you are *making* yours," he says. Indeed, people wait to see her pass. They wait at night at the palace, hoping she'll visit the king. But the papers begin to report on things she never did or said. Is it another Margaret Cavendish parading down London's streets? On another peculiar outing? In another ridiculous dress? That night she dreams she's eating little silver fish; each time one fish goes in, ten more come sliding out.

In the morning she tells Lucy she will only sit and read. But she's promised to visit her sister—so another gown, the carriage, another ride to read about in the papers the following day.

Catherine in middle age looks remarkably like their mother, her hair pulled back as their mother's always was. Margaret's own hair is freshly reddened, curled. She might see herself in her sister, yes, but her sister seems so real. How pleasant is the glow of Catherine's little room. "How nice this is," Margaret says, and takes a bite of cake. Then all at once her sister's grandchildren arrive. How simple. How sweet it is. "This is the Duchess of Newcastle," Catherine says. The children stare with their bright, round eyes. Margaret shifts in the chair. My hat is too tall, she thinks.

Outside, the day is hot.

"It'll be out of the way," her driver says.

But Margaret doesn't care.

So rather than east on Holborn, they sweep down Drury Lane, all the way to Fleet Street, around the remains of what was once St. Paul's—it's here she brought her *Poems & Fancies* in 1652, to Martin & Allestyre at the Sign of the Bell, now burnt to the ground—up Old Change to Cheapside to Threadneedle to Broad. At last she sees the gates. Here is Gresham College. She raps and the driver stops. But as she steps from the carriage, she sees the street is burned. It's black beneath her boots. At once she remembers William's words, as if she heard them only now: The Royal Society of London no longer meets at Gresham, damaged in the fire. Then what is she doing here?

As she stands, a crowd begins to form.

On the corner, a sign: a unicorn means an apothecary's shop. Margaret begins to cross the street. But a hackney coach's iron wheels come screeching across the stones. She presses herself against a wall. A woman stands beside her, a screaming child slung across her back. When was the last time Margaret walked such streets alone? She opens the door—the shop is dim—but she cannot simply stand there as the apothecary stares. So back into the street, quickly to the carriage. The driver helps her up. The crowd has grown. They point and call, "Mad Madge! Mad Madge!" and mud hits her window as the driver takes a left.

So, it comes. And there's nothing she can do, even as she feels it come and wishes that it wouldn't. *Mad Madge! Mad Madge!* she hears in her head all night.

At dawn, Lucy fetches William and tells him about the crowd. William sends for the doctor. She is only half asleep, half dreaming of that coach, screaming, the screaming baby pressed against the wall. She wakes to the awful shadows of the bed curtains on her arm. "Well," the doctor says, "no harm was done." And William—good William—kisses her cheek. Has she been forgiven? He holds her hand as she lies there, bleeding into bowls. When visitors come to the house, the butler tells them the duchess is indisposed. William stays until the doctor's real cure arrives, a stinking ointment that Lucy has been instructed to spread on her mistress's legs. "It will open sores," William explains, "so that the harmful humors might be expelled." Her hands in waxed gloves, Lucy spreads the salve. Margaret faints from pain. She oozes onto sheets.

Near dawn each day the roosters shout.

At night she hears the bells.

A pattern of days and nights.

Of birds, then bells.

Finally, one afternoon, William leads her to the yard. Her legs are mostly healed. "I think we should have a party," he says, reaching around to steady his wife. She holds a green umbrella. "To refresh you," he goes on. The cool air stirs the sores beneath her skirts. "It will be only those friends we've known for years," he says. "Your sister, and Richard Flecknoe, and Sir George Berkeley and his wife."

The ladies wear satin dresses, the men thick black wigs. Margaret is prepared: she has Latin for one guest, translation for the bishop, sea nymphs for Sir George's wife. They drink out on the lawn. But the bishop is ill and does not come, and she is seated next to Sir George and not Sir George's wife. Margaret passes a platter of eels, a calf's head eaten cold, as Sir George offers a chilled silver bowl with a salad of burdock root. His hands are faintly shaking. "Had you heard," he loudly says, "I am now an official gentleman member of London's Royal Society?" "No," she says, straightening in her chair, "I had not heard." "Well, well," he goes on, "you made quite a stir, my dear." Her *Blazing World* was passed from man to man. "Quite ruffled," he laughs, "quite ruffled." Who was ruffled, she wants to know. But William is asking the old man for news, so Margaret repeats her husband's question in Sir George's ruddy ear. And with another laugh, he begins to tell of a recent meeting in which Sir Robert Moray gave an account of an astonishing grove—in Scotland? was it Wales?—its trees encrusted with barnacle shells. "Inside the shells," he says and chews, "when Moray pried them with his knife, what do you think he found?" He looks the length of the table, for everyone listens now: "Miniature seabirds!" he says. "Curled up and still alive!" The party is delighted. The table shines with light. Margaret watches the salad go, its shining bowl and tongs. But who was ruffled, she wants to know. "Tell us of Robert Boyle," Catherine's husband says. "Is it true he walks with a limp?" "You think of his colleague Robert Hooke. A sickly man, though gifted." "A great man," someone says. "Then who is Moray?" "Sir Robert Moray," someone says. "Pardon me," says Margaret, and everyone turns. "Forgive me," she says, "but we had been speaking—that is, Sir George had been speaking of my recent book, of comments made at the Royal Society, and not of Sir Robert Moray or Robert Hooke and his limp. You see," she says, as everyone watches, "I have lately felt a great desire—that is—I would very much like to present my ideas. I would like to speak to the Royal Society. I would like to be invited."

In Margaret's *Blazing World*—with its river of liquid crystal, its caves of moss, and bears—the young lady, inevitably, marries the emperor and, as empress, eventually, begins to feel alone. After the wedding night, she scarcely sees the emperor. Months pass. She has a son. She rarely sees him either. Lonely and bored, she appoints herself the Blazing World's Patron of Art and Science, names the Bear-men Experimental Philosophers, the Ape-men

Chemists, the Lice-men Mathematicians, and calls a convocation of the Bird-men, her Astronomers, instructing them to instruct her in the nature of celestial life.

"A Sun," begins a bird with a prominent crest, "is a vast bigness."

"Ah, yes?" she says.

"It is yellowish and splendid."

The empress agrees it is all of these things.

"A Moon," he continues, "is whitish and dimmer. But the great difference between them is that the Sun shines directly, whereas the Moon, as can be perceived on any moon-shiny night, never respects the center of our world."

"What of sun-motes," she asks. "I've long been curious about those flecks that stir in the air."

"Nothing but streams of small, rare, transparent particles, through which the Sun is represented as through a glass, thinner than the thinnest vapor, yet not so thin as air."

"Are they alive?" she asks.

"Yes," says the bird, shaking his crest. "They must be alive, for they are visibly nourished by the presence of the Sun."

"And what is the air, exactly? A creature itself?"

Another bird stands, plumed in yellow and gray.

"Empress," he says, "we have no other knowledge of the air but through our respiration. Nature is so full of variety, our weak senses cannot perceive all the various sorts of her creatures."

"Quite so," she tells him, pleased.

But the Bear-men annoy her with their microscopes, their artificial delusions, and she orders them to break the instruments, each and every one.

Walking back to the palace, crossing a canal, the lady thinks about wind. It was wind that brought her to the Blazing World, or else its peculiar lack. How odd it is that one winds up where one does. Was she born to be an empress and not a bird or a girl? She carries on like this for quite some time.

"Are seeds annihilated when a plant grows?"

"Is God full of ideas?"

"Is lightning a fluid?"

"Is thunder a blast of the stars?"

Until, one quiet day, having run out of questions, the empress is ready to share her ideas. She asks the spirits to send her a friend, one chosen from among the greatest modern writers: "Galileo," she says, "Descartes?" But the spirits assure her these men would scorn to be scribes to a woman, and they suggest instead an author called Margaret Cavendish, who writes, they tell the empress, nothing but sense and reason. Thus, with a bang of air and a puff of wind, the soul of Margaret Cavendish is brought into that world.

The carriage jerks to life.

They'll make much of what she wears—a gown embroidered with glass Venetian beads, red-heeled shoes, a cavalier's hat, an eight-foot train, a man's black *juste-au-corps*—a completely peculiar hybrid. One member will even mistake her for a man, until he sees her breasts. Yes, much will be made of her appearance, though she doesn't know it yet. Just now, in the carriage rushing down John Street, she doesn't know—what they will say, what she will say—and she tries to assemble her thoughts, fixed in one point, like a diamond.

Her thoughts spin out instead.

There is so much she might say: about indeterminacy and contradiction, about multiplicity and shifts and turns, about what if, and what if, and who knows, and fairies supping on ant eggs—who knows!—and amazing desirable shapes, deer made of oak and running through the woods, and men made of sycamore writing poems on papery chests, their arms "may be like spreading Vines, Where Grapes may grow, soe drinke of their own Wine."

Traffic is thick and a line of boys pursues her in her carriage.

Then, once again, the carriage is off, at two o'clock on a damp gray afternoon. Can a life be said to have a point toward which it moves, like a carriage down a London road, or rainwater in the gutter headed for a drain? At two o'clock on a gray afternoon? But no, she thinks, a life is not like that. They pass a merchant with a long white beard. A pamphleteer with pamphlets. When the carriage stops at the crossroads, she sees a man on a platform claim he can make the time stand still: "And away we go! Away we go, ladies and gentlemen! Clap your hands! Away we go!" But before she can see what happens, the carriage jerks ahead.

Has the time stood still?

The carriage stops; it starts again.

She could take back her request and decline their invitation. She could knock and tell the driver to turn right on Fetter instead. But here are the gates of Arundel House. Here is the Royal Society's dictum: *Nullius in verba*. Take no man's word for it. A crowd in the street pushes and stares. "Mad Madge!" she hears as the gates swing wide. She does not turn her head.

In the formal yard: Lord Brouncker, Sir George, the Earl of Carlisle. They bow as she descends. Beyond the lords, the gates. Beyond the gates, the crowd: "Mad Madge! Mad Madge!"

Brouncker leads her in and down a darkened hall. It smells of powdered wigs and snuff, much like the house in Paris where she used to sit and listen. But a person cannot be in two places at one time, and she is here, not in Paris. She sees a skeleton in a corner. A jar alive with bees. Then Brouncker stops, so Margaret stops. They stand before a door. "It is the first time the Royal Society has beheld a lady in its congress. The room is full," he says. "Everyone has come." Margaret nods, adjusts her hat. She follows him through the door.

The meeting has begun. She watches as they watch her sit. The air is cold, the windows tall. The walls are blue and hung with portraits. The table is polished and square—she's always imagined it round—and in benches on three sides sit the famous philosophers and gentlemen members alike. She sees their wigs and eyes, sees an instrument on the table, a piece of raw meat, a glass of something green. And where moments ago, alone in the carriage, it seemed time was rushing ahead, now it seems to Margaret that time is standing still. The moment eddies, pools at her feet. Robert Boyle. Henry More. John Evelyn. Christopher Wren. What will she say? How will it start?

Then the focus shifts. A man steps from the crowd. "Robert Hooke," the secretary says. Indeed, she sees, he limps. "The air pump," Hooke announces. He measures the weight of the air. A globe-shaped magnet is pulled through iron filings. A slice of roast mutton is immersed in a liquid and immediately turns to blood. He displays one instrument after another, hardly pausing between. It's clear he has performed this before. For other aristocratic visitors, other invited guests? Indeed, many of the men look bored as two round marbles are by machinations flattened. He does something with a compass. Something pretty with prisms and light.

London's bells begin to toll; an hour has passed, though she's not yet spoken a word. Now Hooke places a microscope on the table. Their brittle art, she's called it. He asks her to look inside, observe the swimming bodies. All the faces turn to her. Margaret looks inside—she blinks—a horse neighs in the street. She sees the bodies, swimming, like blossoms on a breeze, like actors in a play, she thinks, in and out of view. The image flickers, suspended. Hooke continues his speech. She shifts her gaze to the bodies that fill the room. Like one body, she thinks, with many pairs of eyes. And a feeling comes over her then, the feeling that she's been walking here across a vast expanse with something in her hands. The image flickers, suspended. Alone, she thinks. I am quite alone. And, thus distracted, she catches only fragments of Hooke's concluding speech—"light, by which our actions are to be guided . . . be renewed, and all our command over all things"— to the serious philosophers and the gentlemen members assembled in the room.

He almost missed the meeting, for bricklayers came to mend a chimney in his kitchen. Yet keen to see her, he hurried all the way. "The Duchess of Newcastle is all the pageant now discoursed on," at breakfast tables and dinner parties, over porridge or pike, she was all that anyone spoke about—or so he'd written in his diary several weeks before. For she was *everywhere* that season. She was at the theater; she was entertaining the king; she was riding down the street. And *everyone* had seen her, yet he could not manage to spot her. So when it was rumored the Duchess of Newcastle would repay the king's visit the following Monday, he'd loitered at Whitehall Palace well into the night, the palace packed with eager visitors, as if it were Christina, the Queen of Sweden, at any moment expected. But the duchess did not appear. She awaited an entire new livery for her footmen—or so the papers said—all of silk velvet, with caps that mimicked the caps of the king's own footmen, a costly and a grand procession, with one coach—the papers said—carrying her gentleman attendants, then the carriage bearing the duchess, then a four-horse coach carrying her ladies-in-waiting, they in gowns of lutestring and she in a fashion of grandeur, heavily embroidered and trimmed in lace, with jewels in her ears, high-heeled shoes on her feet, and a puff of feathers atop her head fit for a masque or a play or a ball, a triumphant show, the court!

It therefore came as a surprise, the following Sunday, to learn that the Duchess of Newcastle's carriage had rolled into Palace Yard with little ceremony, as he, Samuel Pepys, had been at church in Hackney.

He missed her, too, at the annual celebration for the Order of the Garter—the processions, the feasts—she in a flowered gown, a petaled hat of roses, he in the Navy Office dealing with accounts. Then came May Day and the park was like a circus. The air was thick with hawthorns, cakes, and shit. "Mad Madge," someone cried from the crowd, at last. "Mad Madge," someone repeated, as her black-and-silver carriage came roaring down the path. Black stars on white cheeks. "The whole story of this lady is a romance," he wrote in his diary that night.

And so, when Sir George Berkeley announced at a recent meeting of the Royal Society that the Duchess of Newcastle hoped to visit—that he had dined with her at Newcastle House and that she *hoped to be invited*—Pepys, a gentleman member, had been pleased, curious and pleased, even as the news caused a collective groan in the room. They were a new organization, after all, still working to make their name. Putting aside all that she had written—her attacks on their work—there was no telling what she would do. They'd all heard the stories: the crowds, her breasts at the theater, the slight she'd given the queen. They could easily imagine the mocking ballads the next day at the pub. Yet she was a duchess, was favored by the king. Debate followed, pro and con. Until, whether out of loyalty or real friendship to the duke, the aristocratic members urged the invitation be sent.

So she'd arrived, twenty minutes late—so she sits there still.

Hooke has finished and the room awaits her reply. But the duchess only sits, looking into the device. That hat is too much, Pepys thinks—still, her shape is fine. At last, she lifts her head. What ingenious remark will she make? "Gentlemen," she says, "I am all admiration." She rises from her chair. "I am all admiration," she says again. She nods, stiffly, as if wishing them well. She looks to Lord Brouncker, who stands, surprised, and leads her to the door.

"A mad, conceited, ridiculous woman," Pepys writes that night in his diary. She was pretty enough for forty-three, but what a disappointment. She said nothing at all worth hearing. "I do not like her at all."

William sits in a chair beneath the portrait of his first wife, who is quiet as a pearl, the moon. Margaret is quiet, too. She looks peaceful, though she'd returned in a state. "I said nothing!" she'd cried in the entranceway, unsteady as on a ship. "I don't understand," he'd answered, coming to find his wife. She'd wept there on the tiles with her hand against a wall. He'd coaxed her into a chair, persuaded her to take some wine.

She's calm now, exhausted. There was nothing she could have done. It was only a pretty performance. "It was only more chatter," she says.

Once, beside a brook, she'd created whole worlds with the tip of her leather boot. She was Margaret, Queen of the Tree-people, and her brothers had built her castles of ropes in the elms. Something had mattered so much—an argument about a bird? She'd watched her own enormous shadow as she'd marched across the fields.

"They will say I failed or that I'm a fool."

"My dear," William says, "the honor was theirs."

Out in the garden, it pours.

Days later, the Dutch fleet enters the Thames. London panics. The papers move on from the duchess to the war. She and William ride north, in haste. The city slides from view, replaced by farms, then hills, then woods. And though she does not know it yet, she will never leave Welbeck again. She'll continue to read widely, correspond widely, too. She'll write a well-received biography of William, a second book of plays. And she'll pay to reissue her *Blazing World* with its critiques of the Royal Society and its wild fancy intact.

She calls for the carriage. She makes her daily tour. Through the grounds, into the village, past the children, into the woods. The day is nearly done. The sky is a yellowish pink, the snow a mirror, a yellowish pink beneath. Even the village cottages have taken on a glow, sheep like pearls in pinkish snow. Out the carriage window she sees ancient oaks, the wet black earth, and thinks of the orchard in Antwerp—the same black earth, wild and dark, but nothing else is the same. She thinks of the orchard in Antwerp—and she'd been dressed as a bee! "Let's be off," William had whispered, but she'd just then spotted the queen dressed as an Amazon. "Let's get out of this place," he'd said, guiding her through the busy castle and back into the air. There were the stars, still dotting the sky, the lanterns on their hooks. And there was Christina, Queen of Sweden, stepping into a carriage. There was her ankle, her foot. "What a lovely party," said a pretty girl who'd passed them on the stairs.

Now Lucy arrives to prepare her for bed. She unbraids, untwists her mistress's hair. "What shall we speak of?" one lady asks the other. "Aren't they lovely?" says the other of the roses in a vase.

At last she is alone. Another day is done. In her nightgown, in her slippers, Margaret opens the book: "It is a Description of a *New World*, not such as the *French* man's World in the Moone; but a World of my own Creating, which I call the *Blazing-World*: The first part whereof is *Romancical*, the second *Philosophical*, and the third is merely *Fancy*, or (as I may call it) *Fantastical*; which if it add any satisfaction to you, I shall account my self a Happy *Creatoress*; if not, I must be content to live a melancholly Life."

EPILOGUE

ONE WINTER MORNING, SHE WENT OUT FOR A WALK. THE YARD WAS A blank sheet of snow. The sky was curious—more a sea than a sky—and she walked into the woods in breeches and riding boots. When they found her, hours later, she was sitting alone on a garden chair, leaning to one side.

It was 1673. She was forty-nine. She was survived by her husband and her many Paper Bodies. Through them she would live on, she hoped, in many ages and many brains.

William was unprepared. He never imagined he'd outlive her, his blushing, awkward wife. With her body laid out below and villagers filing through, he sat alone in her chamber amid her gowns and books. They lifted her casket into a carriage, which lumbered up the drive.

After resting in the reception hall at Newcastle House one night, Margaret made her final tour through London's clamorous streets. Mourners and the curious followed. No one shouted.

Church bells tolled. Her husband could not be there, too old to make the trip, but her favorite sister, Catherine, walked beside her all the way. She was laid to rest in the Cavendish family vault.

William died three years later, almost to the day.

They are buried together in Westminster Abbey. The inscription above their bodies reads: "Here lies the loyal Duke of Newcastle and his Duchess, his second wife, by whom he had no issue: her name was Margaret Lucas, youngest sister to the Lord Lucas of Colchester, a noble family: for all the brothers were valiant, and all the sisters virtuous. This Duchess was a wise, witty and learned lady, which her many books do well testify; she was a most virtuous and a loving and careful wife, and was with her Lord all the time of his banishment and miseries, and when he came home never parted from him in his solitary retirement."

AUTHOR'S NOTE

This is a work of fiction. To readers interested in historical biography, I recommend Katie Whitaker's *Mad Madge: The Extraordinary Life of Margaret Cavendish, Duchess of Newcastle, the First Woman to Live by Her Pen* and Kathleen Jones's *A Glorious Fame: The Life of Margaret Cavendish, Duchess of Newcastle, 1623–1673*.

I am also indebted to the writing of Virginia Woolf, which is where—in "The Duchess of Newcastle" and *A Room of One's Own*—I first met Margaret Cavendish, and in whose life and work I unexpectedly found much inspiration for the woman who took shape inside this book. Furthermore, my book incorporates, here and there, lines and images from Woolf's own writing (as well as material from Cavendish's work, of course).

*

Finally, I'd be remiss not to mention the following, which were used to varying degrees in my writing and research:

Ashley, Maurice. *Life in Stuart England*. New York: G. P. Putnam's Sons, 1967.

Barker, Felix and Peter Jackson. *London: 2,000 Years of a City and Its People*. New York: Macmillan, 1974.

Battigelli, Anna. *Margaret Cavendish and the Exiles of the Mind*. Lexington, KY: University of Kentucky Press, 1998.

Bowerbank, Sylvia and Sara Mendelson, eds. *Paper Bodies: A Margaret Cavendish Reader*. Ontario, Canada: Broadview Press, 2000.

Bryson, Bill, ed. *Seeing Further: The Story of Science & the Royal Society*. London: HarperPress, 2010.

Campbell, Mary Baine. *Wonder & Science: Imagining Worlds in Early Modern Europe*. Ithaca, NY: Cornell University Press, 1999.

Clucas, Stephen, ed. *A Princely Brave Woman: Essays on Margaret Cavendish, Duchess of Newcastle*. Aldershot, UK: Ashgate, 2003.

Danielson, Dennis Richard, ed. *The Book of the Cosmos: Imagining the Universe from Heraclites to Hawking*. Cambridge, MA: Perseus Publishing, 2000.

Daston, Lorraine and Katharine Park. *Wonders and the Order of Nature*. New York: Zone Books, 2001.

Hartley, Sir Harold, F.R.S. *The Royal Society: Its Origins and Founders*. London: The Royal Society, 1960.

Hazlehurst, F. Hamilton. *Gardens of Illusion: The Genius of André Le Nostre*. Nashville: Vanderbilt University Press, 1980.

Hunt, John Dixon. *Garden and Grove: The Italian Renaissance Garden in the English Imagination: 1600–1750*. Princeton: Princeton University Press, 1986.

Inwood, Stephen. *The Man Who Knew Too Much: The Strange and Inventive Life of Robert Hooke, 1635–1703*. London: Pan Books, 2003.

Keen, Mary. *The Glory of the English Garden*. Boston: Bulfinch Press, 1989

Leasor, James. *The Plague and the Fire*. New York: McGraw Hill Book Company, Inc., 1961.

Orsenna, Érik. *André Le Nôtre: Gardener to the Sun King*. Trans. by Moishe Black. New York: George Braziller, 2001.

Pearson, Thesketh. *Merry Monarch: The Life and Likeness of Charles II*. New York: Harper & Brothers, 1960.

Peck, Lynda Levy. *Consuming Splendor: Society and culture in seventeenth-century England.* Cambridge: Cambridge University Press, 2005.

Pepys, Samuel. *The Diary of Samuel Pepys, Volume VII, 1666.* Edited by Robert Latham & William Matthews. Berkeley: University of California Press, 2000.

Plumptre, George. *Royal Gardens.* London: Collins, 1981.

Sarasohn, Lisa T. *The Natural Philosophy of Margaret Cavendish: Reason and Fancy During the Scientific Revolution.* Baltimore: The Johns Hopkins University Press, 2010.

Scott, A. F. *Every One a Witness: The Stuart Age.* New York: Thomas Y. Crowell Co., 1975.

Stafford, Barbara Marie and Frances Terpak, eds. *Devices of Wonder: From the World in a Box to Images on a Screen.* Los Angeles: Getty Research Institute, 2001.

Tinniswood, Adrian. *By Permission of Heaven: The True Story of the Great Fire of London.* New York: Riverhead Books, 2004.

Turner, John Grantham. *Libertines and Radicals in Early Modern London.* Cambridge: Cambridge University Press, 2002.

Weld, Charles Richard. *A History of the Royal Society: With memoirs of the presidents, Volume I.* London: John W. Parker, 1848.

ACKNOWLEDGMENTS

Short excerpts from this book appeared previously in *Vanitas*, *Western Humanities Reviews,* and *Birkensnake*. Thank you to their editors. Thank you to my lovely agent, Cynthia Cannell, and my incredible editor, Pat Strachan. To Andy Hunter, Julie Buntin, Jennifer Abel Kovitz, and everyone at Catapult. To my earliest readers and advisors, J'Lyn Chapman, Kathryn Davis, Gregory Howard, John McElwee, Miranda Popkey, Suzanne Scanlon, and Kate Zambreno. To W. Scott Howard for *Paper Bodies*. To Washington University in St. Louis, and my colleagues in the English Department, for time and support. And above all, to my forever reader, the wise and patient Martin Riker, for Elijah and everything else.

ABOUT THE AUTHOR

Danielle Dutton is the author of a collection of prose pieces, *Attempts at a Life*, and a novel, *SPRAWL*, which was a finalist for the Believer Book Award. She also wrote the text for *Here Comes Kitty: A Comic Opera*, an artist book of collages by Richard Kraft. Her fiction has appeared in *Harper's*, *BOMB*, *Fence*, *Noon*, and other periodicals. Dutton, who grew up in Central California, holds a Ph.D. from the University of Denver and a M.F.A. from The School of the Art Institute of Chicago. She is the founder of the publishing house Dorothy, and teaches at Washington University in St. Louis, where she lives with her husband and son.